FORTUNE'S WHEEL

A CLAIRE ROLLINS COZY MYSTERY BOOK 4

J. A. WHITING

Copyright 2017 J.A. Whiting

Cover copyright 2017 Susan Coils at www.coverkicks.com

Formatting by Signifer Book Design

Proofreading by Donna Rich

This book is a work of fiction. Names, characters, places, or incidents are products of the author's imagination or are used fictitiously. Any resemblance to locales, actual events, or persons, living or dead, is entirely coincidental.

All rights reserved.

No part of this publication can be reproduced or transmitted in any form or by any means, electronic or mechanical, without permission in writing from J. A. Whiting.

To hear about new books and book sales, please sign up for my mailing list at:

www.jawhitingbooks.com

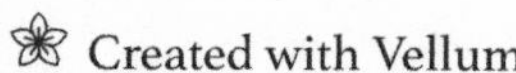

For my family with love

1

On the beautiful September morning, a line of customers had formed out the door and along the sidewalk waiting to get into the North End chocolate shop. Ever since Nicole, Claire, and Robby won the grand prize in the Boston Summer Food Festival the chocolate sweets could not be produced fast enough and sold out almost every day.

Nicole, thirty years old with long, dark hair and brown eyes, was the owner of the shop and she had to be reminded frequently that too many customers was a good problem to have.

When there was a lull in the action, thirty-five-year-old Claire Rollins, an employee in the shop and a friend of Nicole's, stepped out from behind the counter to clean the tops of the unoccupied café tables and sweep the floor.

Claire glanced over to where Tessa Wilcox sat at a table in the corner of the shop with another woman. The two had their heads together in an earnest conversation and Claire noticed some colorful cards spread out on the table between them.

Moving to clean off a vacant table by the window, Claire was about to push aside a newspaper that was left behind by a customer until a headline caught her eye, *Mysterious Murder of Cambridge Graduate Student Still Baffles Police*, and she paused to scan the article. After reading the first paragraph, Claire, with a cloth in her hand, sank down onto the chair, engrossed in the story of the nearly thirty-five-year-old murder.

Sandy-haired Robby Evans, a part-time worker at the shop and full-time college student, paused next to Claire after delivering a latte to a man seated by the windows. With his hand on his hip, he said, "Sitting down on the job I see."

"Huh?" Claire raised her eyes and pushed a loose strand of her curly blond hair from her eyes. "Oh, this article is...." She pointed at the headline. "It drew me in. It's a really odd case."

Robby took a look at the newspaper and after

reading the headline, he stepped back with a shudder and raised his hand with his palm towards Claire. "No thanks. No cold cases. Present day life has more than enough crime and intrigue for me." The young music student had recently been involved in a murder case that Claire and Nicole had been sucked into. "Which, just so you know, I would like a break from criminals and murderers."

"Yeah, okay," Claire said automatically, not really paying attention as her mind was keenly focused on the story she was reading. When Nicole came over a few minutes later and sat at the table, Claire didn't even notice.

"Claire," Nicole said.

Claire pulled herself away from the story and looked up. "I didn't hear you sit down." She slid the news article over to her friend. "Take a look at this. It's about a cold case from years ago. A graduate student was murdered in Cambridge. The case has some weird elements to it."

Nicole glanced warily at the newspaper. "What kind of weird elements?"

"The woman, Leslie Sanborn Baker, was a second year graduate student studying for her Ph.D. in archaeology. She was found bludgeoned to death in her apartment. She wasn't sexually assaulted, no one heard any screams, nothing was stolen, and, get this, there was red powder sprinkled around the room and on the body."

"Red powder?" Nicole's nose scrunched up.

"Yes," Claire leaned forward, the blond curl falling back near her eye. "No one has ever been accused of the crime. The reporter mentioned in the article requested the case records, but the District Attorney's office refused."

"Why would they refuse?" Nicole tilted her head.

"Good question."

Nicole said, "Cold cases like these often benefit from files being released. New information gets discovered. Sometimes, the crime is even solved because the release of the file information brings in new evidence."

"That's exactly the point being made in the article." Claire pushed the paper closer to Nicole.

Nicole read the first few paragraphs and then looked up at Claire with a surprised expression. "The guy in the story, Marty Wyatt, is trying to get the crime records released. He's a private citizen. Why would he want to do that?"

"The article says Wyatt was a young journalist at the time of the murder," Claire noted. "He was assigned to cover the case. It was one of the first stories he ever reported on."

"I wonder why he's bringing up the case now?" Nicole asked.

"Maybe the story haunts him. Maybe he is upset that no one was brought to justice." Claire noticed that their friend, Tessa, had glanced over to them several times from the corner table and when Claire made eye contact with the woman, Tessa looked away.

"What does the article say about the red powder?" Nicole asked. "What was that about?"

"It reports that there was red powder sprinkled around the crime scene. The powder is called ochre. The story quotes an archeology professor who said the substance was used in ancient Persian burials."

"The woman was studying to be an archeologist?" Nicole asked.

"Yes. She also studied ancient cultures," Claire told her.

"So the killer must have had knowledge of ancient burial practices." Nicole looked alarmed. "Having that knowledge would probably cut way down on the list of suspects."

"Ochre is also used by artists," Claire said. "Leslie

Baker painted, so the powder may have been in her apartment because she used it in her artwork."

"That seems more likely, doesn't it?" Nicole asked.

"And, guess what?" Claire pointed to a paragraph in the article. "Someone else was murdered in the same building complex five years earlier."

Nicole's eyes widened. "Were the two deaths related or was it coincidence?"

"Authorities don't seem to know for sure, but they lean towards the killings being a coincidence."

"Someone should raze that building." Nicole turned the newspaper over so the story was facing down. "Who would rent an apartment in that place? Gosh, the two murdered women didn't rent the same apartment, did they?"

"It didn't mention anything about that."

Nicole shook her head sadly. "It's a strange world, isn't it? Thirty-five years ago, the same terrible things that are going on today were happening back then."

Claire let out a sigh. "It's sad to say, but these kinds of things have been going on throughout human history."

"And unfortunately, things don't change," Nicole said with a groan.

The woman Tessa had been taking with gathered her things, smiled, said a few final words to Tessa, and then left the shop. Claire looked over at the table and met Tessa's eyes. The auburn-haired woman lifted one of the cards and held it up for Claire to see.

Nicole stood up. "I'm going to start the next batch of the caramel-swirl brownies."

"I'll be there in a second." Claire nodded to her friend. "I'll unload the dishwasher and then get going on the macarons."

When Nicole disappeared into the back room, Claire crossed to Tessa's table with a smile. "I see you're trying to get my attention."

Tessa, in her late fifties, pointed to the tarot card that had an eight-spoked wheel in the center. The god, Anubis, rose from the right side of the card and a snake descended on the left. Four symbols, one in each corner, represented the elements of earth, wind, fire, water.

"Wheel of Fortune," Claire read the words along the bottom of the card. Looking at it made her heart skip a beat.

"This card can mean different things depending on where it comes up in a reading and which cards are around it." Tessa did tarot readings for people as a part-time occupation and had also helped Claire better understand her strong intuitive skills. Ever since her husband died, Claire could sometimes pick up information about a person by touching them or shaking their hands. She could also sense things from situations and her ability was so strong that Tessa classified it as paranormal.

Tessa said, "I think of this as the wheel of the Roman goddess, Fortuna, the goddess of luck, chance, fate. Who knows how the wheel of fortune will land? Life can bring prosperity. It can also bring disaster." Tessa locked eyes with Claire.

"Why are you showing me this?" A shiver ran along Claire's skin.

"You need to remember that the wheel can bring change and no matter what that change may be, you can handle it with reason, strength of character, and a stable sensibility."

"Is change coming?" Claire asked as apprehension tugged at her.

"What you were reading about in that newspaper...." Tessa turned the Wheel of Fortune card over. "It's floating on the air in here. It might try to suck you into it and if it does, you will need to be strong. You will also need to be very careful, Claire."

Trying to brush off the idea of danger, Claire

gave a shrug. "I don't know how it could drag me into it. It was just a story about an old murder case."

When Tessa tilted her head to the side and her face took on a skeptical expression, her dark auburn curls bounced around her face. The woman had nearly flawless skin and perfect white teeth. "What case is it? Did it happen in Boston?"

"In Cambridge. A graduate student was killed. It was a long time ago."

Tessa's jaw muscle tensed as the color drained from her face, but before she could speak, the door to the chocolate shop opened and Claire's boyfriend, Detective Ian Fuller, walked in with a grave expression on his face. When he spotted Claire, he headed over to her with slow, heavy steps.

Ian greeted Tessa and gave Claire a hug. "Do you have a few minutes to talk? I have a favor to ask you ... Nicole, too."

"Is everything okay?" Claire put her hand on Ian's arm, worried about the concerned look in his eyes.

"I just want to talk to you about an old cold case."

The little, blond hairs on Claire's arms stood up. "A cold case?"

Ian said, "It's starting to get some new attention. A guy I know asked me to have a look at the information he's gathered on the crime. Since you and Nicole have been helpful on recent cases, I'd like to talk to you about this one."

"Sure." Claire's heart began to race. "Nicole's working in back. I'll go get her."

"Thanks." Ian's face brightened. "I'd like to get your input."

Claire started for the back room, but turned back to her boyfriend. "Who's the guy who asked for your help?"

"Marty Wyatt. He used to be a journalist."

Marty Wyatt was the man mentioned in the newspaper article as the young journalist who covered the murder of Leslie Sanborn Baker over three decades ago.

Claire's throat tightened as she took a quick look at Tessa.

Fortune's wheel was turning.

2

When a crowd of customers came into the chocolate shop, it was decided that Nicole and Ian would meet at Claire's townhouse for dinner so Ian could share information about the cold case. Claire's apartment was located in a small neighborhood of historic brownstones known as Adamsburg Square at the edge of Beacon Hill. The neighborhood consisted of several cobblestone streets with brick walkways and old-fashioned streetlamps.

Claire's townhouse had a large living room with three enormous windows and a sliding glass door that opened to a small garden with a rectangle patch of lawn, two shade trees, and a brick patio all enclosed by a high white fence. The townhouse also had a large dining room, a renovated, high-end kitchen, two bedrooms, and a small private basement.

Claire's rescue Corgis, Bear and Lady, rested in the grass while the three people sat on the patio finishing their dinner of chili, corn bread, rice, and salad. When coffee, tea, and chocolate-swirl cheesecake were brought out, Ian placed a folder on the outdoor table and they got down to business.

Ian said, "Marty Wyatt worked as a journalist for a couple of years before going back to school for a master's degree in public policy. He's worked as a consultant in government and business and teaches college courses. I met him about six years ago when we both served on a government task force. He's a good guy." Ian paused and took a long swallow of his coffee and when he set down the mug, he let out a sigh. "Marty recently got some bad news about his health. He only has about a year left."

Claire's eyes filled with sadness. "The poor man."

"How old is Marty?" Nicole asked.

"He just turned fifty-five. Marty's been haunted by the death of the young woman. He wants to try and solve the case before he dies and if he isn't successful, at least he'll have brought the case back into prominence which might help someone else find the killer."

"Is he sure he wants to spend his last year on something so terrible?" Nicole asked.

Ian gave a slight nod. "I asked him the same question. Marty wants justice for the woman. He wants to use the time he has left to find the person responsible for her death."

"We read the article that was in the newspaper today," Claire said. "There are a lot of strange aspects to the case."

Ian said, "You read that the DA's office won't release any of the records? It's been thirty-three years, but they will not give up any of the case information."

"Is that unusual?" Claire questioned.

"Not really. Not in this state, anyway. The DA's office doesn't want to jeopardize any possible future prosecution by releasing details publicly. Should someone ultimately confess, the authenticity of that confession could be questioned if information that only the killer would know has been made public."

"That makes sense," Claire said. "But, it's been so long. Wouldn't releasing some of the information help the case? The DA's office wouldn't need to reveal everything, but a few pieces of information might spark people to come forward with what they knew."

"That's the argument being made by Marty," Ian told them. "He has appealed the decision to withhold. He isn't hopeful, which is one reason he's asked me to look over what he knows." Opening the folder, Ian shuffled through some papers until he found what he wanted. "I'll give you a summary of his case notes. You might know some of it already from reading the article in the news. The victim was twenty-three-year-old Leslie Sanborn Baker. She was working on her doctorate in archaeology and was supposed to take a final exam on the day she was found murdered. Her boyfriend, Peter Safer, went to the apartment around noon to ask how the exam went and he discovered the body."

Nicole let out a groan. "How terrible."

"There isn't a clear motive for the crime," Ian went on. "There was money on the dresser, three hundred dollars in cash, but it wasn't touched. No valuables were taken. Not a single person reported hearing any screams or noise of a struggle. In fact, there were no signs of struggle in the apartment so investigators surmise that Leslie was asleep when the intruder broke in or she knew the killer and willingly let the person in."

"She was found in bed?" Claire asked.

"Yes, she was found in bed wearing a nightgown with the blankets pulled up around her." Ian checked his notes. "In addition, there was a coat, a small, rectangular rug, and two other blankets piled on top of her covering her head."

A shiver of anxiety rushed through Claire's veins. "Why would someone do that?"

"There are theories, but nothing definitive. Some think it might have been a symbolic act of burial. Others say it may have been because the killer felt remorse and didn't want to see the young woman's face. There could have been other reasons."

"There was something in the article about red powder in the room," Nicole said. She told Ian what they'd read in the news about the powder being sprinkled around the bedroom and on the body.

Ian said, "That's right. The professor who originally suggested the idea that the powder may have been spread around the room to recall ancient burial practices, would not discuss the issue again with journalists."

"Why not?" Claire asked.

Ian made eye contact with Claire and Nicole. "Maybe the head of his department suggested he keep quiet so as not to bring suspicion on anyone associated with the college's department."

Claire's eyes widened and she sat up. "*Did* suspicion fall on anyone in the department?"

"Suspicion fell on a number of people, but nothing stuck."

"Who was considered a possible suspect?" Nicole asked.

"Some friends, the boyfriend, neighbors. It also could have been random."

"A random killer seems unlikely though, doesn't it?" Claire asked. "Considering the objects piled on the woman's head and the sprinkling of the powder, don't those aspects of the case make a random killer kind of a stretch?"

"The powder may have been in the apartment from Leslie's art work," Ian reminded them. The killer may have delighted in performing some ritualistic acts as a display of power. The killer may not have known that what he or she did with the powder after killing Leslie was related in any way to ancient burial practices."

Claire sighed and went inside to get a glass of craft beer for Ian and a bottle of wine and two glasses for her and Nicole. The white lights she'd strung between the trees sparkled in the darkness and she lit a few of the tin lanterns around the small yard before patting the dogs' heads and returning to the table.

"Before we hear more about crime scene details and suspects, can you tell us anything about what Leslie was like?" Claire asked. "Is there any anecdotal information about her as a person?"

Ian flipped through a few pieces of paper in his folder. "Leslie was bright, energetic. She played tennis, she loved to paint and draw. People described her as friendly, helpful, cheerful, fun. She sincerely cared about others. She volunteered to tutor elementary school kids and she volunteered with a group that made visits to the elderly. Leslie loved reading about history and learning about ancient civilizations."

"Any siblings?" Nicole asked.

"Leslie was an only child," Ian said.

Claire asked, "Are her parents living?"

"Both are deceased."

"What did the parents do for a living?" Claire questioned.

"They were both professors. The father was a researcher in chemistry at the university and the mother was a mathematics professor at a college in Boston."

"Did the parents live in Cambridge at the time their daughter was killed?" Nicole asked.

"The family home was in Arlington," Ian reported.

"How was the relationship between Leslie and her parents?" Claire asked.

"I remember reading in the notes that the family had a warm relationship."

Nicole said, "The newspaper article stated that a woman was murdered in the same building complex a few years before Leslie's murder. Could the two killings have been related? Might the same person be responsible?"

Ian said, "The initial answer to that was no, the same person probably did not kill both women. The first woman, Denise Pullman, was thought to be a victim of a serial killer, Anthony Bender."

"But...?" Nicole asked.

"But that may be incorrect. A few years ago, the body of Mr. Bender was exhumed and DNA tests linked him to the murder of one of the twenty victims of the suspected serial killer. Authorities are still unsure who killed Denise Pullman. Law enforcement leans towards Bender, but there isn't any hard-fast, conclusive evidence which makes a lot of people think Bender did not kill Denise Pullman. I *do* believe he was the killer of Ms. Pullman."

Claire ran her finger over the side of her wine glass. "Did Leslie have any enemies? Were there any run-ins with someone? Did someone bear her a grudge or did anyone feel slighted by Leslie in some way?"

"There was a guy who wanted to date her, but Leslie wasn't interested." Ian swirled the beer around in his glass. "There was one other thing."

Claire and Nicole leaned forward slightly.

"It seems that Leslie and a professor may have engaged in an affair," Ian told them.

"An affair?" Claire's eyes went wide. "With a professor?"

"Leslie was involved in an affair with one of her professors?" Nicole's mouth hung open.

"It wasn't someone she took a class with. It was a professor from another university. She met him on an archaeological dig."

"Was this just rumor?" Claire asked.

"At the time, a couple of people mentioned it to detectives. The professor denied it, of course. It's something to keep in mind."

"How old was the professor?" Nicole questioned.

Ian glanced at the notes. "The man was new to

his department. He'd been hired two years prior. He was thirty-one-years old when he was on the dig with Leslie. His name was Malden Ambrose."

"That would make him sixty-four now," Claire observed. "A lot of people who were around at the time of the crime must be in their fifties, sixties, or seventies. Some might have passed away."

"Which makes it all the more maddening that the DA's office won't release any of the records," Nicole said. "The killer could very well be dead."

Bear and Lady whined and got up from the grass. They headed to the table where Lady put her nose against Ian's leg and Bear pushed his head under Claire's hand for a patting.

Ian closed the folder. "If you're willing, I can make copies of Marty's notes for you to read. We can get together again to go over anything you find odd or have a question about. I'd like to get your impressions about what the notes say ... does anyone stand out to you as suspicious, are there things that seem like they don't add up, anything like that."

"You think we can help?" Nicole asked with a touch of surprise in her voice.

"You both seem to have strong intuitive skills. I'd like to get your take on the information. It certainly can't hurt."

Claire and Nicole agreed to read through the notes.

Ian cleared his throat. "There's something else I'd like to ask you to do."

A sensation of anxiety caught in Claire's throat.

"Marty tells me that the person renting Leslie's former apartment is moving out. I'd like to visit the place." Ian's brown eyes looked from Claire to Nicole. "Would you come along with me when I go to see the apartment?"

Despite the crime having been committed so long ago, the idea of visiting the murder scene made Claire's heart sink.

"I'll go with you," Nicole told Ian.

Ian looked at his girlfriend and took her hand. "Claire?"

"Okay, I'll go along," Claire said softly. She could feel the murder case pulling at her and the sensation of it made her want to run ... far, far away.

3

Located three blocks from Harvard Square, the building complex that Leslie Baker lived in nearly thirty-three years ago wasn't really a complex at all. It was a triplex of brick buildings on College Avenue with short brick walkways leading to the three main doors on the first floors. There were flowering bushes and colorful flowers blooming in beds around the perimeter of the buildings, each one four stories tall.

Claire, Nicole, and Ian stood on the sidewalk and stared up at the third floor.

Ian said, "Leslie's apartment was on the third floor at the rear of the building. There are four apartments on each floor running along a hallway accessed by the front and back staircases. Thirty-three years ago, the place was in rundown condition. The locks on the main doors didn't work. Leslie's neighbors told police that the door to her apartment hardly ever locked properly so most of the time, Leslie didn't even try to lock it."

"Sheesh," Nicole said. "What terrible security."

"Years ago, it wasn't uncommon for people to leave their doors open and unlocked," Ian said. "Now, it would be remiss to be so cavalier about personal safety. It's a changed world." Pulling a set of keys from his pocket, he held them up. "The renter has moved out so we have access to the apartment. Ready?" Ian led the way inside.

As Claire took another look up at the third floor windows, she let out a sigh and stood straight, silently repeating to herself there was nothing to worry about.

Just inside the small entryway, a staircase stood in front of them, and slightly to their left, there was a small elevator that could hold four people if they squished together.

"I'll walk," Claire said after getting a look at the tiny elevator. Ian and Nicole agreed.

At the landing on the third floor, Ian pointed out

the door to Leslie's former apartment. "Two graduate anthropology students, both women, lived in the apartment across the hall, another graduate student lived alone in the front place and across from him, there was another grad student, a young man."

"Were they all students in the anthropology department?" Nicole asked.

"Yes, they were." Ian placed the key in the lock, turned it, and pushed open the door. "Here we are."

They walked into the empty living room, a rectangular space with three windows that faced the rear of the building. The wood floors were in need of polishing, but the room had high ceilings and a nonworking fireplace stood on one wall. A kitchen was off the living room in a tiny alcove and a short hall about eight feet long led to a small bedroom and then to a bathroom.

"A fire escape runs along the living room and the bedroom just outside the windows," Claire observed, trying to stay focused and attempting to ignore the growing sense of dread that threatened to overcome her. Her heart beat like a sledgehammer against her chest wall. "I don't suppose these windows were locked since the doors were never locked either.

Someone could have snuck up the fire escape and come in through one of the windows. It's doubtful the person would have been seen. It was after midnight, at the back of the building. It would have been easy to gain access without being noticed."

All of the rooms were empty of furniture and a bit of dust had gathered in the corners of the spaces. Ian and Nicole walked around getting a feel of the place. Claire couldn't shake the eerie feeling from being in a room where a murder had occurred. Her head started to pound and she wished she hadn't agreed to come.

"Was Leslie strangled?" Nicole asked. "We never did finish reading that newspaper article."

Ian said, "Leslie was on the bed on her back. She'd been bludgeoned to death. She had deep lacerations at the back of her head. Initial suggestions were that she'd been attacked with a hammer, a rock, maybe a small hatchet. She may have been asleep on her side or her stomach when they attacker struck or she may have been sitting up and was hit from behind."

"If the attacker came in with a weapon, then the murder was premeditated," Claire said. "Did Leslie keep a hammer or a hatchet in her room? Did anyone look into that?"

Ian said, "She kept a few tools in her room that she'd taken on archeological digs, but the medical examiner reported that the injuries could not have been made with those tools, and anyway, they were all present and accounted for and none of them had any blood on them."

Claire crossed her arms over her chest. "So someone came in here carrying a weapon with the intent to do Leslie harm."

"It seems so."

"What about the people who lived on this floor with Leslie?" Nicole asked. "Was she friendly with them?"

Ian gave a nod. "Leslie was on a dig the prior summer with one of the residents. The woman's name is Amy Wonder. She lived across the hall from Leslie with a roommate. Amy's boyfriend, Henry Prior, lived on this floor in one of the front apartments. All of the students reported being friends, or at least, friendly. Amy's roommate, Jill Lansing, was often at her boyfriend's apartment on the other side of Harvard Square and wasn't around much."

"Was Jill here that night?" Claire asked.

"She was here when Leslie arrived home from a date with her boyfriend. Leslie stopped by their apartment to chat for about thirty or forty minutes.

Amy's boyfriend, Henry, was there, too. Jill reported that she left the building about thirty minutes after talking with Leslie in order to go to her boyfriend's place for the night."

Claire said, "So Leslie went out on a date and when she returned home, she stopped by Amy and Jill's apartment to talk. They chatted, Leslie went to her own place, and thirty minutes later, Jill left the building to go to her boyfriend's apartment. Is that right?"

"That's what the notes say." Ian ran his hand over his short, brown hair.

"No one reported hearing signs of a scuffle or a struggle or any screams?" Nicole asked.

"That's right." Ian put a hand in his suit jacket pocket. "So Leslie was either asleep when the attacker hit her or she knew the person and was sitting on the bed when she was hit."

"People probably were coming and going in this building all the time," Nicole noted. "With so many students living here, there must have been people visiting all the time, there must have been parties, there must have been music playing, people must have gathered together often to study. It might have been a noisy place. Maybe that's why no one heard anything or they didn't pay any attention if there was some noise."

"Good points," Ian said and then looked over to Claire who was standing at the threshold to the bedroom.

"It's strange, isn't it?" Claire asked. "Luck ... fate, how the world turns. Would Leslie have been killed if she'd leased a different apartment? Did someone take offense to some minor remark she made and planned to kill Leslie because of it? Did a man become enraged because she wouldn't date him or because she broke off with him? Encounters, interactions, running into the wrong person, being in the wrong place at the wrong time, it can all have major consequences, but we hardly ever think about such things."

Nicole let out a sigh. "We'd never leave the house if we thought about every little thing. We wouldn't be able to function."

Claire turned to Ian. "You mentioned that Leslie went out on a date that night. She was seeing a young man, right? Was he the one she was out with the night she was killed?"

"Yes, the young man was from England. His name is Peter Safer. They'd dated on again, off again for almost two years. Some people referred to Peter as Leslie's boyfriend, other people called him her friend." Ian walked to the bank of windows and looked out. "I don't know if Leslie would have referred to her going out with Peter that night as a 'date'. Maybe they were out together as friends."

"Do you know what they did that evening?" Nicole asked.

"They went out for pizza and then they stopped for a drink at a pub where they ran into some friends."

"The police must have interviewed Peter extensively," Claire said. "They didn't consider him a suspect?"

"Oh, they did," Ian said. "Peter told detectives he walked Leslie home. She had her exam the next morning so he didn't want to keep her up late so he said goodnight, wished her good luck, and headed back to his apartment."

"Did anyone see him? Did he have roommates?"

"Peter Safer lived alone. No one in his building saw him return home. Peter said he went home and watched a movie, then went to bed."

"And what about the people in Leslie's building," Claire asked. "Jill left the building shortly after Leslie went to her own apartment. What did Amy and her boyfriend do after that? What was their story?"

"After Jill left, Amy Wonder and Henry Prior made some fried eggs and toast, watched a little television, and then Henry went back to his place."

"They heard nothing out of the ordinary?"

"Nothing," Ian said. "At least, that was their claim."

Claire tapped her chin with her index finger. "Leslie was supposedly having an affair with a professor then? Was it still going on at the time of her murder?"

"That depended on who you talked to," Ian said.

"Did Leslie's boyfriend know about the affair?" Nicole asked.

"Supposedly not. Peter was said to be shocked when the investigators brought it up. The young man said it wasn't true and that some jealous person made the whole thing up to make Leslie look bad."

"Someone must not have liked Leslie very much if they'd make up a story like that." Claire absent-mindedly twirled a lock of her hair around her finger. "Did that person dislike Leslie enough to kill her?"

"Too many questions, too many suspects, and too much time has passed since Leslie was killed."

Nicole rubbed the back of her neck. "How could anyone solve this so long after the fact?"

"It's possible," Ian said. "It's happened before. Crimes have been solved years later. Sometimes, many years later."

"Are people still around who were here at the time of the murder?" Claire asked.

"Some, yes."

Claire's mind was trying to process all the details. "Is your friend, Marty, talking to them?"

"He has, yes."

"And it hasn't been any help?" Claire asked.

Ian shook his head. "Not so far."

Claire glanced around the empty bedroom. What went on in here? Who killed you? Why did he do it? How did he get away with it? A flash of anger raced through Claire's body.

Ian's friend, Marty, was so distressed that no one had been brought to justice that he hoped his last acts on earth would help point to the killer. Claire didn't want any part of the case ... she did not want to get involved, but standing in the room where Leslie was killed and thinking about Marty yanked at her heart strings.

Although the weight of the sadness pressed hard against her and she wanted nothing more than to flee the building, Claire could sense answers floating on the air, silently moving past her like ghosts from the past ... answers that were still available to be found. She knew she had to help. With slumped shoulders, she turned and reached for Ian's hand. "Someone knows something ... but someone isn't talking."

Yet.

4

"That girl had everything, didn't she?" Nicole asked as she and Claire walked through the square on their way to pick up the subway. "She was attractive, intelligent, was getting her doctorate from a prestigious university, was headed for a wonderful career." Nicole gave her head a shake. "I guess she had everything except good luck. Life sure can be cruel."

"Isn't that the truth." Claire thought about losing her husband and about the victims of the crimes that she and Nicole had recently been drawn into.

"We're going to get involved with this one, aren't we?" Nicole glanced at her friend. "I can feel your hesitation, but I know how things will go. We'll get pulled into it even though we prefer not to be."

Giving a shrug of her shoulder, Nicole said, "We have to do it. We both believe in using our skills for good."

"Tessa warned me about this." Claire rubbed at her temple.

"Did she?" Nicole sounded alarmed. "When?"

Claire shared Tessa's concerns with Nicole. "She said we have to be careful."

"Oh, no. I thought we'd be safe because the case is so old. Everyone involved with it is middle-aged or older." Nicole groaned. "We need to think about this rationally. Does it really matter if this case gets solved? Is there anyone around who cares anymore? Leslie's parents are dead. She had no siblings. There's no one left."

"What about Marty Wyatt?" Claire asked.

"Maybe he should let it go. He's in ill health. Maybe he should spend his days doing things he enjoys. Does Leslie Baker really need justice done? She's gone. Her friends are either dead or old."

"People in their fifties aren't old. I was married to someone in their seventies," Claire reminded Nicole.

"Oh, you know what I mean. Leslie's friends have lived for a long time without the murderer being caught. Is it worth all the time and effort this will take, especially if it will put us in danger?"

"What if the killer is still alive?" Claire eyed her friend.

Nicole stopped walking and looked at Claire with a frown. "I didn't think about that."

"Would that make a difference?"

"I guess it would," Nicole muttered. "The killer should go to prison. He lived for thirty-three years after robbing Leslie of her future. He's had his whole life." Nicole straightened. "If the killer is alive, then yes, it would make a difference. I'd want him to go to jail."

"We won't know if the killer is alive until we help Ian and Marty with the case."

"You're right." Nicole didn't look happy about it.

"Ian can't do a whole lot," Claire said. "He's a full-time detective and his department doesn't want him actively working this case, but he can act as a consultant. I think that's why he asked us to read through the notes and give our impressions. So we can help his friend. Ian will set up a meeting so we can get together with Marty and see what needs looking into. I feel obliged to help for a bunch of reasons. First, because Ian asked. Second, it's important to Marty. And third, because someone stole years from Leslie's life and shouldn't get away with it."

Nicole asked, "Where do you think we should start?"

Claire said, "If people are still living in the area, I'd like to talk to the boyfriend, Peter Safer, and the people who lived in Leslie's building."

"Peter Safer may have returned to England after he completed his degree."

"Let's hope not." Claire held up her hand and crossed her middle and index fingers for good luck.

"What about that professor Leslie was rumored to be having an affair with? What was his name?"

"Malden Ambrose. He was working at a different university than the one Leslie attended," Claire recalled.

When they walked by a coffee shop, Nicole suggested they get a drink and sit outside in the warm, September sunshine.

Sipping their lattes, Nicole did a search of Professor Ambrose on her phone and after a minute, she lifted her eyes with a triumphant grin on her face. "Guess who still works at a university in Boston?"

Claire smiled. "Really? Then after we meet with Marty, let's plan on paying Professor Ambrose a visit."

"The woman who lived in Leslie's building and

was murdered a few years before ... what was her name? Denise?"

"It was Denise Pullman. She was studying for a master's degree. I don't remember in what field."

Nicole tapped at her phone and after a few minutes, she said, "Denise Pullman was an elementary school teacher. She was studying for her master's degree in education. The article reports that she was stabbed four times. It mentions the shabby condition of the building and that the door's locks were basically useless."

"I guess the owner of the buildings didn't care to improve safety for the residents since the locks were still awful five years later when Leslie lived in the complex."

"That person should have been jailed for negligence." Nicole put her phone on the table and when she raised her drink to her lips, she nearly dropped the cup, but saved it by catching it with the palm of her other hand.

Her eyes were wide and she was staring down the block. "The bakery owners who co-won the food festival grand prize with us, Jim and Jessie Matthews, just walked across the street. I've seen them twice before and when they notice me, they give me such mean looks. I think they hate me."

"It doesn't matter. They can't stand the fact that they didn't win the prize alone." Claire smiled. "They must not like to share."

"They give me the creeps. When they glare at me, I feel sort of, I don't know ... unsafe."

"If you run into them again, just ignore them," Claire suggested. "Before work tomorrow, I'm going to stop in at Tony's Market. I want to talk to Augustus about Leslie Baker's murder. He must know or have heard plenty about the crime since he was already a judge in the lower courts by that time."

Ninety-one-year-old Augustus Gunther lived in the Beacon Hill neighborhood of Boston and had served as a lawyer and a judge all of his working life. The judge knew a good deal of the city's history and was acquainted with many people in and out of both the court system and law enforcement. His knowledge and experience had come in handy over the past months and Claire hoped to pick his brain over this murder case.

"That's a great idea," Nicole said. "I bet he'll know some details and may have heard some rumors that might be helpful. What does your intuition tell you about whether or not Leslie was killed by the same person who murdered the teacher, Denise Pullman, five years prior?"

"I don't think they're related." Claire gave a shrug. "I don't know why, but it's the feeling I get. If we try to connect the two deaths, I think we'll be wasting time and nothing will come of it."

Nicole raised her eyes to Claire. "Did you pick up on anything when we were in the apartment?"

Claire put her elbows on the table, leaned forward, and lowered her voice. "I have to admit I was uncomfortable in there thinking about what happened years ago. My mind felt unfocused like it was jumping from thing to thing. I was nervous, agitated. I wanted to get out of there." Claire's face was dead serious. "But things are still floating on the air from long ago. I could feel them nudging at me. Answers are out there. It's not too late. We just have to find them."

"You don't look happy about it."

"We need to be careful, Nic. This could be a bad one. Things about this case have been hidden for a very long time. I get the feeling that someone wants the information to stay buried and would do just about anything to keep it that way."

"You're scaring me." Nicole grasped her hands together.

"We need to pay attention to everything. We need to be aware. We can't take any chances."

"You sound like Ian when he lectures us." Nicole tried to lighten the mood.

Claire gave a half-smile. "This time, I'm taking the lectures and warnings to heart."

"Okay." Nicole took in a deep breath. "We'll be on guard."

Claire voiced her worries. "I think we need to be careful about who we trust and what we believe. People are going to try and push us down the wrong path. We'll be lied to. After reading the notes, I have a million questions for Marty. What stymied this case? Was it police mishandling of the evidence and suspects? It seems students and friends weren't interviewed in a timely way and after the body was discovered, the neighbors had access to Leslie's apartment and bedroom ... they went in and out ... the police didn't secure the place for hours."

Nicole asked, "And why did that professor who discussed the ochre at the crime scene and suggested that the killer may have been recreating ancient burial practices stop talking to reporters? He wouldn't say any more about it. Did someone tell him to stay quiet? If someone did, why would they do that?"

"This is how we'll get some answers, by asking all the right questions." Claire forced a smile. She needed to stay positive even when panic pounded through her veins. Feeling like she and Nicole were about to step off solid ground into quicksand, Claire wondered which way Fortune's wheel would turn for them ... would it be success ... or would it be disaster?

5

Claire was carrying a brown pastry box as she opened the door for the Corgis to enter Tony's Market and Deli. In his early seventies, tall and burly with a full head of white hair, Tony Martinetti had owned the Adamsburg market at the edge of Beacon Hill for over fifty years. He'd taken a shine to Claire and her dogs when they moved to Boston and now considered her a part of his family.

"Morning, Blondie," Tony called from behind the counter before stepping out to greet his favorite dogs.

Bear and Lady rushed over to dance around the man and each one received pats on the head and a dog treat before they clicked over the floor to the rear of the shop to find Judge Augustus Gunther sitting at one of the small café tables reading the newspaper and sipping his cup of coffee.

Claire gave the big man a hug.

"What do we have here?" Tony indicated the box.

"I brought some lemon cream muffins and a chocolate-banana bread." Claire opened the box and Tony removed a muffin, lifted it to his face to sniff, and closed his eyes. "Ahhh, lemon."

Claire chuckled and, as was her usual early morning habit, she headed to the back of the shop to sit with Augustus and have a cup of tea. The Corgis had already greeted the judge and scooted through the back store room to the small, wall-enclosed garden where they spent the day until Claire returned from working at the chocolate shop.

"Ian talked to me about a cold case a friend of his is investigating." Claire opened the bakery box and placed the sweets on a paper plate she took from the coffee and tea counter next to the café tables.

Augustus's light blue eyes shifted from the newspaper propped on the table to Claire. "Did he?"

"His friend was a public policy consultant for many years and recently retired."

"Marty Wyatt." Augustus folded the newspaper

and set it to the side. "I heard the man has received some bad news regarding his health."

"You know Marty?" Claire asked.

"We're acquainted with one another." Augustus adjusted his navy tie. The former judge wore a suit and tie every day no matter what the weather. "He seems like a good man."

"You know the case he wants to have reopened?" Many times, Claire had been impressed with the judge's sharp mind and she hoped he would recall this case.

"I know it." Augustus gave a slight nod. "A most unfortunate incident."

"There must have been a lot of chatter and speculation around the time it happened," Claire said.

"Quite a bit, yes." The judge raised his cup to his lips. "Is Ian planning to work on the case?"

Claire explained that the department didn't want Ian spending time on the old case. "He'll go over things with Marty and act as a consultant."

"And what would Ian like you to do?" Augustus's face was serious.

"Nicole and I are going to meet with Marty. Maybe we'll talk to some people who knew Leslie Baker, if they're still in the area." Claire put a slice of the banana bread on a small paper plate and handed it to Augustus before removing a slice for herself. "Are you able to share some things you know or remember about the case?"

"Some things." Augustus bit into the bread and complimented Claire on her baking skills. "Why don't you ask me questions and I'll see if I can provide an answer."

"Was there a prime suspect?" Claire asked. "Was there someone law enforcement suspected, but didn't have enough evidence to make an arrest?"

"Not to my knowledge."

"Did the police mess up the evidence?"

"Possibly. My understanding is that the scene was not contained quickly enough, that people, neighbors and friends, came and went for a couple of hours before police locked down the apartment."

"Was that how things were done back then or was it negligence?" Claire asked.

"They should have kept people out of the apartment. Evidence may have been contaminated, things were moved around, something was even taken from the bedroom."

Claire's eyes narrowed. "By the police, you mean?"

"Not by the police. By a neighbor. It was a

hammer that Miss Baker took with her on expeditions. She'd been to Spain and to Iraq to work on archeological excavations. She may have worked on other digs, but those are the two I recall."

"Why would the police allow someone to remove an object from the crime scene?" Claire couldn't believe how lax the initial investigation had been run.

"It shouldn't have happened," Augustus said. "In fact, a year later, the object was retrieved from the person who took it."

"A year later? A lot of good that did." Claire couldn't believe her ears. "What if that hammer had been used as the murder weapon? It would have been well-cleaned by the time it was retrieved, fingerprints would have been wiped off and other fingerprints would be on it. That's ridiculous."

"I agree."

"Was it done deliberately?" Claire sat up straight. "Did the police allow the hammer to be taken in order to protect someone?"

"The first police officers who arrived on the scene didn't think anything was wrong with allowing the neighbors into the rooms. They were Leslie's friends, they said, so their prints would have been all over the rooms anyway. The police also allowed people in because they wanted to know if anything was missing from Leslie's place."

"It's outrageous." Claire's blue eyes flashed. "What if one of the neighbors or one of the friends killed her? Any of them could have lied about things being stolen or not, any of them could have moved things around or taken things from the room."

"Yes, but that's how it was," Augustus said. "It did not help the investigation."

"Did suspicion fall on the boyfriend?" Claire asked.

Augustus said, "He was certainly a suspect. In cases such as this, my first thoughts go to a husband or a boyfriend. The police also take first looks at the murdered person's partner. I remember that this young man was a citizen of another country, was it England?"

"That's right. His name was Peter Safer."

"The young man claimed to have walked Miss Baker to her building and shortly after, he went home. I believe Miss Baker had an exam the next day. Mr. Safer told police he didn't want to keep his girlfriend out late because of the exam. There was something about the young man's claims that didn't sit right with me. It was something subtle, but I can't recall what it was, although I do remember being suspicious about what Safer said."

"Did you think he didn't go home right away? Did you think he stayed at the apartment?"

"I'm not sure. I'd have to read over the notes and news article from the time to jog my memory."

Claire said, "I read in the notes Ian gave me that Safer told police he went home and watched a movie, but no one saw him go into his building. He had no one to corroborate what he said he did that night."

"What did Miss Baker do after arriving home?" Augustus asked.

Claire told him that Leslie had visited her neighbors and then went to her apartment.

"Yes, that's right. I recall reading that the bedroom windows were unlocked. There was a fire escape right outside the windows. No one heard screams or a scuffle or shouting. What does that tell us?"

"Either people are lying or Leslie was asleep when she was attacked."

"Or she knew her attacker, perhaps invited him in, chatted with him, and suddenly the person made his move and struck her. It would have been fast, so fast that Miss Baker did not have time to cry out."

"Could someone have made it up the fire escape without being detected?" Claire asked. "The person would have had to pass by the first and second floor apartment windows. The person would be in sight of anyone walking past the rear of the building."

"It was late though," Augustus said. "Hardly anyone would be behind the building at that hour."

Claire said, "But it's taking a chance to climb up the fire escape. You never know when someone might walk by. I don't think the attacker came up that way. The doors on the building were always unlocked. Leslie's apartment door was unlocked. Just walk in and go up the stairs."

"It seems the sensible thing to do, and the easiest."

"What about the murder weapon?" Claire said. "The killer must have planned the killing in advance, don't you think? He must have had a weapon with him when he arrived."

"Unless he used the excavation hammer."

"Was it too small to kill Leslie? Do you think it was a possible murder weapon based on the description of the wounds?"

"My first reaction would be to say no. Since it

wasn't that large, I think there would have to be more blows to the head to cause death, but only a medical examiner or a doctor could give a definitive answer."

"My first impression was that the murder was premeditated," Claire said.

"I might be inclined to agree with you, but I will reserve judgment."

Claire asked, "What about the ochre that was spread over the body and around the room?"

"If it was done to symbolize an ancient burial rite, why would someone do that?" Augustus asked. "Not many people have such knowledge. Why would a person do something like that since it would narrow the suspects down to very few people?"

Claire thought it over. "Maybe it was done in a rage ... without thinking of the consequences? The powder might have been in the room since Leslie was an artist. The killer spotted it and spread it around on impulse." Claire looked at Augustus. "If you were taking up the investigation of the case now, who would be important to interview?"

"Mr. Safer," Augustus replied quickly. "The neighbors. Any close friends. And the professor whom Miss Baker was rumored to be having an affair with."

Claire smiled at the judge. "You have a remarkable memory."

"This murder stuck with me. It was all over the news. It was the talk of the town, everyone giving opinions and discussing the details. I remember much of it as if it were yesterday. There are some cases like that. They stay with you for decades."

"This one didn't end in an arrest," Claire said. "It didn't go to trial. What made it stick with you?"

Augustus looked off across the room, his thoughts moving back over the long years. "Something didn't seem right about it. There seemed to be a sudden lock on the information. The story faded away quickly."

"Someone was being protected?"

"It's a possibility, but don't focus solely on that. Police chase information that doesn't pan out, evidence doesn't hold up, leads dry up. Sometimes cases go nowhere."

"The DA's office still won't release any of the records," Claire told Augustus. "Not one little piece."

"Interesting," the judge said narrowing his eyes.

"Isn't it?" Claire asked.

"I'll ask around. See what comes up in conversations." Augustus looked at the young woman across from him with a serious expression and issued her a warning. "You must be very careful with this one, Claire. The killer hasn't been found out for three decades. He or she would want to keep it that way ... and might be very, very determined to remain undetected. Stay safe."

6

Claire and Nicole arrived earlier than usual at the chocolate shop to make truffles, chocolate and caramel turtles, a variety of muffins, a cheesecake, and mini strawberry shortcakes before their meeting.

As they slipped the last tray of muffins into the oven, they heard the tinkle of the front door chimes and hurried out to greet the man.

Marty Wyatt was about five foot eight inches tall, with short gray hair and a bald spot, and a very thin frame. His skin was pale and had a slightly pasty look to it. Claire and Nicole introduced themselves and the three sat at a table with coffee, tea, and muffins.

"Thanks for meeting with me," Marty said. "Ian

told me how you've been helpful with several cases recently."

"Ian holds the theory that people open up more readily when talking with private citizens than they do with the police," Claire told the man. "In some cases, I think he might be right."

Nicole said, "We've found that people have confided some things to us they didn't share with the police."

"I'm hoping that will be the case in this instance." Marty had pale blue eyes with a bit of droop in the lids making it seem as if he hadn't slept well in a while. "If you'd be willing to speak with some people related to the case, I'd be very grateful."

"We'd be happy to," Claire assured the man.

"Ian must have given you my background, but I'll share some details. After I graduated college, I accepted a job as a reporter and my first important assignment was to cover the Leslie Baker case. When I arrived at the building in Cambridge, there was police tape around the entrance and I couldn't go inside. I talked to another reporter who got in before the police secured the premises."

"We read in the case notes that it took quite a long time for law enforcement to secure the apartment," Claire said.

"It's true. The reporter I talked to told me some of the neighbors had been in and out of the place, people were touching things. He was surprised the rooms didn't get secured sooner."

"The boyfriend and one of the neighbors found the body?" Nicole asked.

"Yes. Peter Safer was the one who found Leslie. When he went in, he saw blood on the wall and Leslie on the bed and then rushed to the neighbor's place and pounded on the door. Only Amy Wonder was at home. She accompanied Safer back to Leslie's bedroom where they lifted some of the things she was covered with, saw the blood and some of the injuries, and knew she was dead. They called the police, but not until they alerted Amy's boyfriend, Henry Prior, who also went into the bedroom to see what had happened."

"Why did they wait to call the police?" Claire asked. "Were they sure Leslie was dead? Did they touch her? What if she was unconscious, but still alive? I know it wouldn't have helped in this case, but why dawdle? Why not call for help in case there was a slight chance Leslie might have been able to be saved?"

"I suppose the delay in calling could be attributed to shock." Marty held tight to his coffee mug. "We don't know how we'd react in an emergency like that. Maybe the mind shuts down and you can't think straight. Maybe the scene was so unbelievable that Peter Safer needed confirmation from someone else that what he saw was really so."

Claire considered Marty's explanations and agreed that they were plausible, although something about Peter's need to get Amy and then Henry before making the emergency call seemed off to her.

"The case has stayed with me my entire life." Marty looked at the coffee in his mug as the muscles in his jaw tightened. "I worked as a reporter for another year and a half and then I gave it up. I couldn't do it. It didn't fit my personality. All the bad things, chasing after and reporting on others' misfortune didn't sit well with me. I followed the Leslie Baker case and when no one was arrested, it broke my heart. It seemed impossible to me that someone wasn't found out. How could someone get away with the murder?"

Marty's face was pinched with emotion. "Leslie was only a year older than me when she was killed. I knew things like that happened often enough, but somehow her death horrified me. It threw the fragility of life right in my face."

Claire had the urge to hug the man, but remained in her seat.

"I didn't want to have kids," Marty went on. "I was too afraid that something terrible would happen to them. I even went to a therapist to get help ... it didn't really help me, but my wife wanted to be a mother and deep down I wanted a family so despite my fears, we went ahead. We had twins, a boy and a girl. The lights of my life. Believe me, I watched those kids like a hawk. Stayed up nights worrying about them. I still do. I'd give my life for those two." When Marty looked up at Claire and Nicole, his bottom lip quivered. "I guess Leslie's parents must have felt the same way about their daughter."

Claire gave the man an empathetic nod. "I'm impressed with your dedication to finding Leslie's killer. Nicole and I will do whatever we can to help you. What would you like us to do?"

"I appreciate it." Marty collected himself. "I've petitioned and appealed to have the decision by the district attorney's office not to release any of the information and files on the case overturned. This could go back and forth for months, or longer, and I'm sure Ian told you that I don't have a long time to battle this by continuing to make appeals. It would be helpful if you could talk to some people who were around back then. Leslie's boyfriend, Peter Safer, is living in the area. Amy Wonder works in a museum in the city and Henry Prior has a position at a Boston hospital. Malden Ambrose, the man who was rumored to have had an affair with Leslie, is a professor at a Boston university. If you could have a chat with the four of them, it would be a great start."

"We'll do that," Nicole told Marty. "Do you have an opinion on whether or not Professor Ambrose was romantically involved with Leslie?"

"I have an opinion, but I won't share it until you speak with him, if you don't mind. I don't want to influence your impressions."

"That makes sense," Nicole said. "We'll go into the interviews with open minds."

"I wonder if these people will be willing to speak with us," Claire said. "They may decline."

"I met with three of them, all except for Peter Safer. He did not want to meet to discuss the case. The man seems to have been reluctant from the start. A month after the murder, the police asked Safer to come in to take a lie detector test, but he wouldn't do it, on advice of his lawyer."

"He never complied with the request?" Claire asked.

"Never."

Claire's forehead furrowed. "Since Safer refused to take the lie detector test, wouldn't that make the police take more careful looks at him? Wouldn't it cause greater suspicion to fall on him?"

"I thought it would," Marty said.

"But no charges were ever filed against him," Nicole noted. "So was he cleared?"

Marty swallowed the last of his coffee. "My guess is that he was never actually cleared of suspicion, but there wasn't enough evidence to charge Safer, so off he went to live his life."

Nicole straightened in her seat and narrowed her eyes. "Did the police try hard enough to solve this case? Safer refused the lie detector test. Why didn't they make him take it?"

Marty shrugged. "They needed more than simple suspicion to force him to take the test."

Nicole blew out a long breath. "The police didn't secure the scene quickly enough, the neighbors and Safer were allowed into the apartment, the body was touched by them, things in the apartment were touched by them, someone took the hammer Leslie used on digs. It was gross incompetence."

"Or was it?" Marty asked with one of his eyebrows raised.

"You think it was something else?" Nicole asked, her mind racing with possibilities.

"Did incompetence permeate the entire investigation?" Marty questioned and leaned forward. "Or was incompetence suggested by someone?"

"Someone who didn't want the truth getting out?" Claire nodded as disgust washed over her. "Who or what was so important that a young woman's murder was brushed aside and buried?"

The expression in Marty's eyes hardened. "That's what I long to find out." The man gave a sigh. "Maybe there really wasn't enough evidence to make an arrest. If that was the way it was, then I'll accept it, but there's been too much hidden and no records will be released. It's been thirty-three years since Leslie was killed. What is the reason the information is being held so tightly?"

Claire didn't like it ... she didn't like it one bit. "Have you ever been threatened because of this case?"

Marty looked surprised by the question. "The answer to that would be no. I've never been directly threatened by anyone because of the case." The man paused for a moment before saying, "If you ask me if I've ever *felt* threatened because I was looking into the murder, then I might have to say yes."

"What made you feel unsafe?" Claire asked with wide eyes.

"After a month on the case for the paper, my editor told me to drop it. He said nothing would come of it. When I protested, he got angry and asked if I wanted to keep my job. There was a cop I used to talk to about the case, he suggested it might be time to let it go. When I asked why, he muttered something about letting sleeping dogs lie and not getting on the wrong side of some people." Marty blinked a few times. "And that's why, after all these years, and after adding up all the parts of this mess of a thing, I can't let it go." With an awful sadness tugging at his face, Marty shook his head. "I just can't."

7

"So Ian thinks you're Clairvoyant Claire, too." Robby frosted the tops of red velvet cupcakes that stood in rows like little round soldiers.

Claire looked up from cutting the pan of brownies into rectangles and gave her coworker the eye. "No, he does not. He wants our input because he doesn't have the time or the go-ahead from his superiors to investigate the cold case."

Nicole piped up from the walk-in refrigerator. "Ian appreciates our intelligence and intuition ... unlike some other people we know."

"I just don't know why Ian would ask two untrained women to look into the murder." Robby leaned down to inspect the last cupcake he'd frosted and then decided to add a little more of a flourish to the top of it.

“Any person can look into a crime,” Claire said. “Marty Wyatt isn’t trained as an investigator, either. Lots of people look into old crimes. There are websites online dedicated to keeping cases alive by discussing aspects of those cases and by gathering information from citizens who spend time trying to find new clues and evidence.”

“Crimes have been solved by these amateur sleuths, you know.” Nicole carried a large box of butter to the work counter. “It’s not poking your nose where it doesn’t belong. It’s volunteering time to help bring justice to the victim, the family, and friends. The police don’t have the time or people-power to take on these old cases. As long as citizen-detectives stay within the law, they’re welcome to do what they can.”

“If someone I loved was the victim of a crime, I’d be forever grateful for any help that regular people could give.” Claire arranged some of the brownies on a white platter for display in the front cases.

“Okay, okay.” Robby put his hands up in a gesture of mock-surrender. “Have at it. Just don’t get yourselves killed.”

Claire glanced over to the young man hard at

work on the cupcakes doing his best to make them look perfect. "We're only going to talk to people, not get involved in a shoot-out."

Robby wiped a bit of frosting from his finger onto his apron. "The killer didn't use a gun so I didn't think a shoot-out was a possibility. It's a knife or a hammer you need to look out for." He walked softly past Nicole and poked his finger in her side causing her to let out a shout.

Robby darted away before she could strike him. "Don't let anyone sneak up on you either," he warned with a grin. "And don't turn your back on anybody."

"I'll remember that." Nicole adjusted her stance at the work table so she could keep an eye on her employee.

"Maybe we should bring you along when we interview some of the people involved in the Leslie Baker case," Claire thought out loud. "We can use you to stand in-between us and the interviewee to keep us safe."

"Sure." Robby lifted a platter of cupcakes to bring them to the refrigerator. "My body guarding rates are pretty high though. I don't know if you can afford them."

Claire chuckled and teased Robby by saying,

"You'd be surprised what I can afford." In fact, what she said was an absolute truth. Her deceased husband had been one of the wealthiest men in America and when he died, his fortune went to Claire who kept a very low profile and when she met with financial advisors or the company leadership, she pulled her long, curly blond hair into a slicked-back bun, wore glasses, and never called attention to herself.

A lawyer by training, Claire ran a tight ship, was a tough negotiator, and didn't allow anything to slip past her at meetings. Her holdings were run on a daily basis by her trusted team who along with Claire, had squashed a hostile takeover of her husband, Teddy's, company right after he died. She and her group had earned the reputation that they were not to be underestimated.

The only person outside of the business community who knew how much Claire was worth was Nicole, and she smiled at the joke to Robby that he'd be surprised at what Claire could afford.

When Robby almost had to drop out of school due to financial pressures, Claire came to his rescue as an anonymous donor so that he could stay in school and finish his degree. Having grown up poor, she was well-acquainted with the hardships and lost opportunities that lack of money could cause and she was determined that no one she cared about would suffer due to financial difficulties.

"So who is your first interview with?" Robby asked.

Claire said, "We're hoping to meet with Leslie's former boyfriend, Peter Safer. Marty gave us the man's email address and I sent him a message requesting a meeting."

"Why would he agree?" Robby added butter to a bowl and was about to cream it with sugar, but didn't switch on the mixer so he could hear the answer to his question.

Claire said, "I told him we were friends of someone with ties to the Baker family. The person wanted to have the case reopened and asked us to help."

"No one will believe that." Robby stood staring at Claire.

"Why not?" Nicole asked with a touch of defensiveness.

Robby raised an eyebrow. "What could you possibly gather that Marty hasn't already put in his file?"

Claire lifted her eyes from her task and looked

over at Robby. "The answer to that question is ... the name of the person who killed Leslie."

"That's a tall order, but I'm not going to say anything negative about the difficulty involved with it. You two have been able to come up with things about cases that eluded the police ... so go for it. Do what you can. Maybe someone will slip up. But really? From what I've read about this case, you might be wading into the deep end of something." Robby looked from Claire to Nicole and before he flipped the switch on the mixer, he said, "Be careful. I don't want to have to run this shop all by myself."

As Robby's mixer whirred into service, Claire and Nicole turned their attention to the work of baking and frosting with their young coworker's words ringing in their ears. Thinking about the details of the case and the people involved, Claire worried that no one would agree to speak with them ... and then, what would they do? Marty would keep appealing to get the DA's records, but how long would it take and what would he learn? If people wouldn't talk, nothing new would ever be discovered.

With a sigh, Claire rolled the last truffle in dark chocolate powder, placed it on the cookie sheet, and carried it to the refrigerator. After washing her hands, she picked up her phone to check her messages.

"Nic," Claire said with excitement. "Peter Safer has agreed to meet with us. Tomorrow. In Downtown Crossing."

"Really?" Nicole hurried over to see the reply with her own eyes and after reading the man's message, she high-fived her friend. "Okay, great. Tomorrow is the beginning of the end."

Claire and Robby looked at their boss with horrified expressions.

Nicole stammered, "I mean the end of the case being cold, not the end of us. Jeez."

"I'm glad you cleared that up. Sheesh." Robby used a spatula to scrape down the batter from the sides of the mixing bowl and headed to the front of the store to retrieve one of the baking tins.

Anxiety pinged along Claire's skin and she had the urge to reply to Peter Safer's message by telling him they could not meet, that the whole thing was a mistake, and she'd never bother him again. The aspects of the case clanged around in her head and her throat felt dry and tight. Hurrying to the sink to get a drink of water, she held the cool glass to her temple and tried to calm herself by taking slow breaths.

As Nicole passed Claire on the way to the ovens, she said softly, "I hope this isn't a mistake."

"We'll be okay," Claire said the words of encouragement as much to convince herself as Nicole. "We're doing the right thing."

"You better ramp up your intuition into high gear by tomorrow," Nicole told her friend. "We're going to need all of your 'skills' on this one. With any luck, we'll find a clue right away that will help Marty figure this thing out."

Luck. Fortune. While Claire wondered which way the wheel would turn for them, Robby poked his head into the back room.

"There's someone out here who wants to talk to you," he said.

"We forgot to lock the front door again," Nicole said with a shake of her head.

With her heart beginning to race, Claire asked, "Which one of us does the person want to talk to?"

"Both of you."

Claire and Nicole exchanged worried looks, pulled off their aprons, and headed to the café section at the front of the chocolate shop.

A well-dressed woman in her mid-to-late fifties with a slim build and short blond hair, turned around when she heard the young women come out of the back work room.

Claire spoke first. "Hello. I'm Claire Rollins and this is Nicole Summers. How can we help you?"

The woman shifted her briefcase to her left hand and shook with her right. "I'm Rosalind Fenwick. I hope I can help *you*."

Confusion covered Claire and Nicole's faces.

Ms. Fenwick made eye contact with them. "I'm an acquaintance of Marty Wyatt. I ran into him last evening. I have some things I'd like to share with you about the Leslie Baker case."

8

As the women took seats near the windows, Robby brought over coffee, tea, and a plate of cookies and set them on the table before scurrying away. Claire and Nicole still had looks of surprise on their faces from the arrival of the unexpected visitor.

"Marty told you we're helping him with the cold case?" Claire asked.

"He did," Rosalind said. "I spoke with Marty years ago shortly after Leslie's murder. I was impressed with his earnest and caring attitude. I was sure the police would solve the crime quickly, but we see how that turned out." The woman sipped from her cup. "I read the recent news article about Marty and his efforts to revive the investigation into the cold case and decided to seek him out."

"Are you planning to assist Marty with the case?" Claire asked.

Rosalind shook her head. "Oh, no. I don't have the time to do that or the first idea of how to go about working on a cold case." Reaching down for her briefcase, she said, "I have some pictures from my time at the university. Leslie is in some of them. I brought them to show Marty. He looked at the photos and asked if I'd bring them by to show you."

"You and Leslie were friends?" Nicole asked.

"Not friends, really. We knew each other from classes and we went on a dig together the summer prior to her death."

"You were studying in the same department?"

"I was studying ancient history and classics so we ran into each other frequently," Rosalind told the young women as she removed several plastic pages from an old photo album she took from her briefcase. Each of the eight by ten plastic sheets had twelve photographs slipped into the insert sections. "These pictures are from my time working on my doctorate. This is the archaeological dig in Iraq we went on together." Rosalind pointed to one of the photos. "This is me and this is Leslie."

Claire and Nicole leaned forward to get a better look.

"It was hot as blazes there. We lived in small buildings with only fans to cool us. We were there for three weeks. I loved the work, but not the high temperatures. The group got along well. Everyone was dedicated and hardworking and we had lots of fun and laughs."

Claire was unsure how the photographs would help the cold case, but she didn't ask Rosalind anything preferring to let the woman continue to present the information in her own way.

After showing the pictures from the dig, Rosalind turned to the second sheet. "These are random photos taken while at the university, at lectures, get-togethers, luncheons, parties. These three photos were taken at a party in Leslie's apartment. If you look closely, you can see a trowel used on digs sitting on the top of the bookcase inside a wooden box with a few other tools. The trowel is unusual because it has mother-of-pearl inlays in the handle."

Rosalind turned back to a photo from the dig she and Leslie had been on. "Here's the same tool on a work table from when we were in Iraq. The trowel belonged to one of the associate professors who worked at the dig. I was surprised to see it in Leslie's apartment."

"Did the professor give it to Leslie as a gift?" Claire questioned.

"I asked her about it. Leslie seemed a little nervous about my inquiry. She told me she liked the tool that Professor Ambrose used in Iraq and decided to buy one just like it for herself." Rosalind made eye contact with Claire and Nicole. "I didn't believe her. Leslie stammered when she replied. She seemed to want to blow it off. Even though she tried to be nonchalant about it, she acted twitchy and nervous. She picked up the wooden cover and closed it over the box."

"Why do you think she acted so nervous about it?" Claire watched the woman's face.

"At the time, I wondered if Leslie had stolen it from Professor Ambrose." Rosalind got a faraway expression in her eyes. "One of the inlays on the handle had a small piece broken off of it. I didn't pick up the trowel that was in Leslie's apartment, but I thought I noticed a corner of the mother-of-pearl was missing so I thought it must be the same one from the dig."

"Do I hear a *but* in your voice?" Nicole asked sensing hesitation in the woman's tone.

"Now I'm not so sure how she came to have the tool. Maybe Leslie didn't steal it. Maybe it *was* a gift from the professor to Leslie."

"Why would a gift to Leslie make her nervous in front of you?"

"I always thought there was an attraction between Leslie and the professor. There were some flirting interactions between them like holding eye contact a little longer than was necessary, brushing their hands together. It was all subtle, playful."

"Do you think they may have been dating?" Nicole questioned.

Rosalind's eyes darkened. "I hope not. When we were in Iraq, Ambrose was recently married."

"Professor Ambrose was on the faculty of a Boston university?" Claire asked.

"Yes, he taught at a college in the city. The dig was a joint project between three universities."

"Is he in any of your pictures?"

Rosalind placed her fingers on two of the photos. "Here he is in this group photo right next to Leslie. I went on another dig that Ambrose was affiliated with. There are other photos from that dig in the later section of the album."

Claire looked at the picture of the tall, slender man smiling broadly at the camera. His left hand was on Leslie's shoulder and her body was turned slightly towards the man with her hand on her hip. Everyone in the smiling group looked confident and self-assured.

Rosalind said, "And here they are in this photograph of all us in front of one of the living quarters."

In the second photo, six people stood in the back row and five others were positioned in the front row. Looking happy and full of energy, Leslie sat cross-legged on the dusty ground in front of Ambrose who was gazing down at her with a wide smile.

"It looks like you had a great time together," Nicole noted after scanning the faces of everyone posing in the picture.

Rosalind let her eyes move over the sheets of old photographs. "There were the expected annoyances and disagreements, but overall it was a wonderful experience."

"Do you know if Leslie kept in touch with Professor Ambrose once they returned from the dig?" Claire asked.

"I don't know. We had a get-together in a restaurant about two months after we came back from the dig. It wasn't obvious if Leslie and Ambrose had seen each other prior to the reunion, but he was flirting with her that night. I got the impression Leslie wanted him to stop. I never asked her if she had been in touch with Ambrose." Rosalind picked up her cup of coffee and took a long swallow. "I was in Leslie's apartment a few weeks after I attended the party at her place, the night I spotted the trowel."

Claire felt a shiver of anxiety move over her skin.

"I went by to pick up a few books I'd lent to Leslie. She was cooking in the kitchen. She let me in and told me her hands were a mess from chopping and said to grab the books from the bookshelf in the living room. While I went to get the books, the smoke alarm went off and Leslie ran back to the stove. The wooden box of digging tools was still on the top of the bookcase. The lid was pushed to the side. I moved it a little more so I could get a look at the tools. I wanted to see the trowel again." Rosalind paused and then said, "It wasn't in the box. It was gone."

"Do you think Leslie needed it for something she was working on?" Claire's mind raced with ideas.

Rosalind's lips tightened. "I doubt it. I think she moved the trowel because I noticed that it was Professor Ambrose's tool."

"Did you share this information about the trowel with the police?" Nicole asked.

"The police didn't interview me," Professor

Fenwick said. "At the time, I didn't even think about the trowel. After reading the news article about Marty trying to renew interest in the case, I pulled out these old photos and remembered seeing the trowel so I met Marty and told him I had wondered where Leslie got it."

"Could a tool like that...?" Claire's inner core felt cold. "Could that trowel have been the murder weapon? When you showed these pictures to Marty and told him what you've just told us, did he think it was possible that the trowel could have caused Leslie's fatal injuries?"

"He acknowledges that only a medical examiner could determine that, but from the things Marty has read and heard about the case, yes, he thinks it could have produced the injuries."

"Did you ever see the trowel again?" Nicole asked.

"I did not. That was the last time I visited Leslie's apartment."

"Did you see Professor Ambrose again?"

"I saw him at Leslie's memorial service. As you can imagine, it was a terrible day. Everyone was distraught that this could have happened to someone we knew."

"Did you speak to Professor Ambrose that day?"

"Briefly. None of us said much except to express our horror and disbelief and share words of comfort with one another."

"Leslie had a boyfriend, Peter Safer," Claire said. "Had you met him?"

"I met him a couple of times." Rosalind shifted around on her seat and sat straighter. "He was at the party at Leslie's place the night I noticed the trowel."

"What did you think of him?"

"He was pleasant enough. I didn't spend any time talking with him and didn't get to know him. Leslie didn't refer to Peter as her boyfriend. She called him her friend."

"Leslie wasn't serious about him?" Nicole asked.

"She didn't seem to be. Leslie was fun and outgoing and eager to learn and have a career. She certainly didn't give me the impression she was ready to settle on any one person." Rosalind tilted her head slightly to the side. "I don't know what Peter thought."

"Do you think Leslie was in a relationship with Professor Ambrose?" Nicole asked the direct question to see how Rosalind would respond.

"I don't know anything about that." Rosalind gave a shrug. "I wouldn't speculate on whether or not they acted on their attraction to each other.

Outside of the dig we were on, I didn't see Leslie on a regular basis."

Rosalind pushed the old photo album towards Claire. "Keep it, if you like. You might want to look at the pictures again. I don't need it back right away."

Claire nodded and then leaned forward. "Did Leslie have any enemies? Anyone who had a grudge against her? Is there anyone you might think of who had a reason to want Leslie dead?"

The corner of Rosalind's mouth turned up. "There were probably a number of people who were quite jealous of Leslie. She was vivacious, intelligent, pretty, fun. There were probably a number of people who wanted to date her, but were unsuccessful in that pursuit. Jealousy, love, unrequited desires ... all are time-tested motivations to kill. Was someone so consumed with any of those feelings that they murdered the woman? Did she know her killer?" Rosalind turned her hands up in a helpless gesture. "I have no idea."

9

Early in the evening, Peter Safer met Claire and Nicole at a pub near Downtown Crossing. The man was tall with broad shoulders and white hair cut close to his head. Well-dressed in a fitted suit, the man looked strong and athletic and his high cheekbones and symmetrical bone structure kept him looking younger than his actual years.

When introductions were made, Safer's posture and handshake seemed stiff to Claire as if the man was uncomfortable or ill at ease. They took seats in chairs at a high table and gave their drink orders to a waiter.

"We appreciate you coming to meet us," Claire said with a smile trying to put Safer at ease.

The man said, “My office is nearby so it wasn't a problem to meet here.”

Claire and Nicole knew that Safer was a very successful financial advisor and in his early sixties, he continued to work full-time. As soon as the drinks arrived, Safer took a long swallow of his whiskey and ginger and drained half his glass.

Claire noticed the drink consumption and hoped if Safer kept on like that, it might loosen his tongue.

“An acquaintance of Nicole's,” Claire fibbed, “is interested in the Leslie Baker case.”

“Why?” A quick moment of annoyance flashed in Safer's hazel eyes.

Nicole said, “He was assigned as a young reporter to the case. He covered the story for a few weeks after the murder. He hopes for some measure of justice for Leslie. We're helping him gather information.”

“What does your friend think will happen after the three of you gather information?” Safer asked.

Claire set her wine glass on the tabletop. “We all hope the case will be reopened and that new evidence will lead to the person responsible.”

Safer smirked and adjusted the cuff of his shirt sleeve. “It's been nearly thirty-five years. People have moved away, some have died. What possible evidence could be left?" A trace of an English accent was evident when the man spoke. "It's a fool's errand, I'm afraid."

"Maybe it is," Nicole said and then moved the discussion in a different direction. "Your career has been in finance? At the time of Leslie's death, you were a doctoral student in anthropology, weren't you?"

Safer shifted in his seat. "I was. I left the program a year after Leslie's murder. I'll answer your next question before you ask it. The reason I left was because academia wasn't for me. I wanted something more financially rewarding so I abandoned the program and went for an MBA instead."

"You've done well, I understand." Claire smiled. "It seems it was the right choice for you."

"I believe it was." Safer didn't smile or make eye contact. He kept his gaze focused on the liquid in his glass.

"You and Leslie dated back in the day?" Claire asked.

"We were friends at times and at other times, we described our relationship as boyfriend-girlfriend. Leslie never really knew what she wanted. Whenever she decided she only wanted to be friends and I subsequently withdrew from her, she'd change her mind and want to get back together. It went on frequently. I felt like a ping-pong ball."

"Did you love Leslie?" Nicole asked.

Safer's eyebrows went up. "I thought I did. In retrospect, I was probably fascinated by her and maybe, a little obsessed with Leslie. She was so enthusiastic about life, so outgoing, friendly. I didn't know anyone quite like her. When she gave you her attention, it was like golden sunshine lighting you up. I've always been a quiet, more reserved person, not shy by any means, but more of an introvert, someone who enjoys books, mathematics, time alone."

"Were you a couple at the time of Leslie's death?" Claire asked.

"We were in transition again. She called us 'friends'."

"Were you annoyed with Leslie's indecision?" Nicole asked.

"Sure I was." Safer made eye contact with the young women sitting across from him. "But certainly not annoyed enough to kill her."

Claire was careful how she worded her next comment. "We've heard some people suggest that Leslie might have been dating a professor."

Safer's face did not reveal any emotion he might

have been feeling. "I've heard the rumors. I don't believe they were true."

"Someone mentioned that Leslie might have had a relationship with a professor named Malden Ambrose."

"No, she didn't." Safer shook his head. "Ambrose was interested in her, but she didn't share his interest."

"Leslie told you this?" Nicole asked.

"She did. Leslie told me about men who wanted to date her, men who flirted with her. I don't think she was trying to make me jealous or anything, she was only making conversation, letting me know what was going on."

Claire wasn't sure if Safer was correct about Leslie's motives for talking about other men and she didn't believe the young graduate student would discuss with Peter a man she was having a relationship with. "Did you know Professor Ambrose?" she asked.

Safer's forehead wrinkled in thought. "I may have met him once."

"He was not affiliated with your university. He taught at a college in Boston."

Safer said, "Yes. Ambrose went to Iraq on the dig expedition that Leslie worked on."

"Leslie reported to you that Professor Ambrose was interested in her?" Nicole asked.

"He was one of many men who was attracted to Leslie."

Claire said, "Someone told us about a trowel Leslie had. It had mother-of-pearl inlays on the handle. Did you ever see the tool? It was used on archaeological digs."

"I know the tool. Leslie kept it in a box with some other equipment."

"Do you know where she got the trowel?" Claire asked.

Safer thought back for a few moments. "I don't know. I assume she bought it along with her other dig instruments. Why do you ask?"

"Did she have the trowel in her possession leading up to the night of her murder?"

"I think she did." Safer's eyes brightened. "She did, yes. I saw the trowel the night I dropped her off. The last time we went out, we had pizza and then ran into some friends at a pub where we had a few drinks. I walked her home afterwards. She had an exam the next day. I didn't want to keep her up late so I was going to walk her to her place and then head home. Leslie asked me to take a look at her stove. She said she thought she smelled a gas leak when she put the oven on to bake so I went up to her apartment to check it out. I saw the trowel in Leslie's bedroom on the book shelf near her bed."

"You remember it being there?" Nicole marveled at the man's memory.

Safer said, "I only remember because Leslie asked me to push her bedroom window up. It was always getting stuck. She liked sleeping with the window open, even in the winter she'd keep it open a crack. I used the trowel to poke under the window to make a space to get my fingers in there to push it up. I always intended to bring over some WD-40 to try and loosen the window in the casing." The man rubbed his forehead. "If I'd left it stuck that night, the killer might not have been able to get in."

"Do you think that's what happened?" Claire asked. "It was an intruder who got into the room through the open window?"

"That's my assumption."

"What happened after you got the window open?" Nicole asked.

"I left and went home."

The last few sentences Safer said had sent shivers of discomfort over Claire's skin. She asked for clarification. "So you left Leslie's apartment as soon as you opened the window?"

"I did."

"And you went straight home?" Nicole asked again.

"That's right."

"Did you head right to bed?"

"I watched a movie for a while and then I went to bed."

"What did you watch?"

"Um ... it might have been ... hmm, I think it could have been an old Hitchcock movie. I think that's what it was, but I might be wrong." Safer's eyes narrowed and his shoulders straightened. "I've told all of this to the investigators. I was not charged with the murder. I don't recall every detail of that night. Perhaps, the passage of time has erased the details from my mind or maybe the shock of the event blocked some of my senses. But, being unable to remember things does not make me guilty. I did not kill Leslie."

"We're not implying that you did," Claire explained with a gentle tone. "We're only trying to get a sense of the time, who Leslie knew, what she was like, who might have done this to her."

"It was most likely an intruder." Safer set his glass of whiskey on the table with a little too much effort.

Claire asked, "Why though? Leslie wasn't assaulted. Her valuables were left untouched. What would have been the intruder's motivation?"

Safer shook his head. "The killer may have seen her coming and going. He may have been mentally disturbed. Maybe the person's only intention was to kill her."

"What about the red powder that was sprinkled over the body?" Nicole asked.

"I don't know the answer to that. Leslie was an artist. I've been told the red powder was used in painting. I didn't know she had it in her place."

"Why would a random killer spread the powder over her?" Claire questioned.

"The killer had to be disturbed. He saw the powder and decided to spread it around the room. The person had to be mentally unstable to commit such a crime. Who knows why someone like that would latch onto the powder? The question is unanswerable."

Is it? Claire wondered.

"So your assumption is that Leslie's killer was a stranger to her, he came in the open window, murdered her, saw the red powder and sprinkled it around the room before exiting back out through the window," Nicole said.

"I think so, yes."

Claire gave a nod. "Did Leslie have any run-ins with anyone? Did anyone have it in for her? Was there someone who didn't like her? Was someone obsessed with her or jealous of her?"

"Probably. Leslie attracted attention. There were men who were attracted to her whom she wouldn't date. There were probably women who were jealous of her looks, her personality, the attention she got from men. Isn't that normal life? People don't usually kill someone because they're smarter or prettier or not interested in dating you. I think its far-fetched to imagine someone killing Leslie because of a grudge. It wasn't some dramatic screenplay we were involved with. It wasn't a movie we were living in."

"You brought up talking to the police investigators," Claire said. "They interviewed you several times?"

"More than once, yes, they did." The muscles near Safer's jaw seemed to tighten.

"Do you think they considered you a suspect?" Claire asked.

"Sure they did. It's common procedure to think the boyfriend did it."

"They didn't make any charges against you."

"That's correct."

"Were you frightened when they questioned you?" Nicole asked.

Safer looked from Claire to Nicole with hard eyes. "A little."

"Do you think your fear could have caused you to hold back any information?" Claire asked.

An angry look flashed over Safer's face and he answered with an almost defiant tone. "No, I don't."

"You feel you answered all of their questions fully?" Claire said.

"Yes, I did."

"The police asked you to take a lie detector test," Claire stated.

Safer stared at her without speaking.

"You chose not to take the test."

"That's correct." Safer sounded like his teeth were clenching.

Claire squared her shoulders. "May I ask why you didn't take the test?"

Safer answered forcefully. "I didn't take the test on advice from my attorney."

"I see." Claire nodded. "Why didn't the attorney want you to take it?"

"He said the test was unreliable. He said the test gave many false positives and many false negatives.

He said the thing was useless and not to subject myself to its follies and whims."

"It sounds like good advice," Nicole said.

Safer glanced at his expensive watch. "If there's nothing else, I really need to get going."

Claire thanked Safer for his time and shook his hand.

When the man was gone, she looked at Nicole. "How come I get an odd feeling from that guy?"

Nicole pushed her long brown hair back from her face. "What kind of an odd feeling?"

Claire narrowed her eyes at her friend. "One that tells me Mr. Safer might be leaving out a few details."

10

With the sun about to dip below the horizon, Claire and Ian strolled hand in hand along the darkening river with the two Corgis walking beside them on leashes. The dogs had their heads down close to the ground sniffing the path and the edges of the grass to find out which dogs and people had walked beside the river that day.

"Do you ever wish you could smell things the way dogs do?" Claire asked Ian with a smile. "It might come in handy for a detective. You could sniff around a crime scene to help determine who had been in the room."

"I never thought about that." Ian chuckled. "Having such a strong sense of smell might be really annoying. I think I'll stick to my conventional methods for crime-solving."

Before heading out for their walk, Claire and Ian had cooked dinner together at her townhouse and sat outside on the small patio enjoying the meal in the shade of the big tree. Conversation flowed easily as they chatted about exercising, what they'd done at work that day, plans for the weekend, how the Red Sox were doing, and current events.

The talk didn't turn to the Leslie Baker cold case until after dessert was finished.

"I guess we have to talk about the case. Tell me about the people you and Nicole have met with," Ian said, the smile disappearing from his face.

Claire had reported who they'd spoken with, but she and Ian wanted to enjoy part of the evening without discussing murder. She told him about Rosalind Fenwick and Peter Safer.

"What did you think of Professor Fenwick?" Ian asked.

Claire put her napkin down next to her plate. "She seemed sincere in her concerns. She told us she hadn't been interviewed by the police. Professor Fenwick was looking at old photos recently and remembered the trowel. She felt it might be important to the case."

"That's interesting." Ian leaned back in his chair and stretched his legs out in front of him. "Leslie may have taken the trowel from the dig site. Sounds like she and Ambrose had a flirtation going on. Maybe the guy gave it to Leslie. I'll look through Marty's case notes to see if the trowel was mentioned. I wonder where it is now."

"Do you think it's odd that Peter Safer recalled unsticking the bedroom window with the tool?" Claire asked.

"Maybe that's what he always did to get the window to go up. Maybe he always used the trowel."

"I don't know. It seems such a minor detail to remember using it after all these years."

Ian said, "Some things are probably burned into Safer's mind. He was interviewed by the police ... most likely, more than once. He had to tell and retell what he did that night. A lot of the details got stuck in his head and are still in there after all these years."

"Too bad you and Marty can't access the interview transcript from back then," Claire said. "I'd like to know exactly what Mr. Safer said in those sessions."

Ian rubbed his chin. "It would be a big help if the DA's office would release *some* information."

"Is Safer married?" Claire couldn't remember if

she'd read anything about Safer having a family. "We didn't ask him about that."

"He was married for about a year in his late thirties and then got divorced. I didn't see anything in the notes about him remarrying."

"He didn't stay married long, did he?" Claire started to feel antsy, like something was picking at her. "I wonder what ended the marriage. It might be interesting to talk to the ex-wife."

"Couldn't hurt."

"What do you think about Safer?" Claire watched the dogs playing with a stick in the grass. "He refused the lie detector test. That makes me suspicious of him."

"His lawyer gave him good advice. The test can produce false positives. Even if the police were suspicious of him, they mustn't have had any hard and fast reasons to pursue Safer. He may be guilty, but ... no evidence, no witnesses, no nothing ... then no arrest."

"I think he's hiding something." Claire frowned. "He's had years to consider what not to say, what to say, and how to say it. He's smooth. He didn't show any feeling or emotion over Leslie's death."

"It's been a long time," Ian said. "Hurt gets

buried. Pain dulls. People learn how to protect themselves from past misery."

Claire crossed her arms over her chest. "Did Safer experience pain when Leslie was killed?"

"Safer's friends and colleagues might be able to give some insight on that question."

"Safer thinks an intruder came in through the window and killed Leslie. He thinks it could have been random or maybe, someone who'd seen Leslie come and go from the building and got the idea to attack her." Claire fiddled with the edge of the napkin on the table. "Is he advocating for this idea because he's trying to protect himself?"

"It's possible." Ian reached down to pat the dogs' heads for bringing him the stick they were playing with. He tossed it across the grass for them to chase. "Or Safer might really believe it was a random killing."

"I don't trust him."

"Is that a preconceived notion you have about the man?" Ian tossed the stick again after the Corgis retrieved it and placed it at his feet.

Ian had no idea that Claire had some paranormal abilities, so she couldn't tell him that she'd had a very strong "feeling" that Safer hadn't been completely honest in his answers to their questions. “My notion is from interacting with the man. Something seemed off. I’d like to talk to people who knew him years ago, a friend, his ex-wife. I’d like to get a sense of Safer by hearing what others thought of him.”

Ian took a swallow from his glass of beer. “Who will you be interviewing next?”

“Nicole and I found Professor Ambrose. He’s still teaching in Boston. We’re meeting with him in a couple of days. We’ve also been in touch with two people who lived in the apartment building on the same floor as Leslie. We’ll be talking to one of them soon.” Claire let out a sigh. “How will we ever dig up something new on this case? We’ll never find any new evidence. The people involved with Leslie have had years to refine their stories. It seems hopeless.”

“It’s only hopeless if we stop looking into it.” Ian held Claire’s eyes. “It’s a heck of a long-shot, but it’s worth a try ... if only to give Marty some measure of peace that he did all he could.”

“You’re right.” Claire gave a nod and smiled warmly at Ian. “We’ll see it through.”

A chilly breeze came over the water and made Claire shiver. Ian moved closer to her and put his arm around her shoulders. The sun set earlier now that it was September and with darkness settling around the couple and the dogs, Claire suggested they turn around and head back to the townhouse for cups of hot tea.

With her mind still working over the discussions with Peter Safer and Rosalind Fenwick, Claire said, "Do you think it odd that Professor Fenwick got in touch with Marty out of the blue?"

"It might have been what she told you, she read the newspaper article, started thinking about the case, thought of the trowel, and decided to bring it up with Marty." Ian held Bear's leash and stopped to wait for the dog to sniff at the base of a tree.

Claire buttoned her sweater against the chill. "If Professor Fenwick thinks the trowel might be the murder weapon, why didn't she bring it up at the time of the murder? She claims her concern about the trowel is a new idea. I don't know if I buy it."

"She might have been afraid to go to the police," Ian said thoughtfully. "She might have thought her idea was silly and didn't want to appear foolish in front of law enforcement."

Claire looked up at Ian. "Do you think the police deliberately ignored evidence in the case? To protect someone?"

Ian let out a long breath. "Mistakes could have been made in handling evidence. And why the investigators didn't speak with people who should have been interviewed, I can't say. It's more likely it was sloppy police work than a conspiracy to hide facts and protect someone, but that sort of thing, although rare, has been known to have happened in other cities."

Bear glanced up at the couple and whined.

"I'd lean towards a fumbled handling of the case," Ian said. "Things weren't followed up on, things slipped through the cracks, things were overlooked."

As they turned off the path by the river onto the street that led to Adamsburg Square, Claire squeezed Ian's hand. "Somebody knows something. I'm sure of it. We just have to find that person and get him to talk."

11

Professor Malden Ambrose preferred to meet Claire and Nicole off-campus at a Boston coffee house. Claire thought it was interesting that both Peter Safer and Malden Ambrose did not want to meet in their offices and chose public places in the city to get together. It was clear that the men wished to distance themselves from the decades-old murder.

Ambrose was over six feet tall with the build of a marathon runner. His hair and beard were light brown with flecks of blond and gray. He wore a golf shirt and tan chinos and stood up when he saw the young women enter the shop.

"Call me Malden." With a wide, friendly grin, the professor shook with Claire and Nicole and gestured to seats around the table. "I hope you didn't mind meeting here. I love the coffee they serve in this place. It's the best in town."

"This was very convenient." Claire returned the man's smile. She could see how people would be attracted to his engaging personality and good looks.

After some general chit chat and questions about Claire and Nicole's backgrounds, the conversation turned to Leslie Baker.

"We heard that you knew Leslie from working on a dig together in Iraq," Claire said.

"Yes. Such a long time ago. Hard to believe. I was one of the organizers of the expedition. We had a great group on that trip. The people around you really make or break how well a dig goes."

"What did you think of Leslie?" Nicole asked after the waiter brought over their coffee and tea.

"Leslie was great." Holding his coffee mug, Ambrose leaned back against his chair in a casual posture. "Intelligent, curious, hard-working, fun. She brought so much enthusiasm to the work. It was infectious."

"So the two of you got along well?" Claire asked.

"We certainly did."

"Did Leslie ever talk about someone who didn't like her, a person who might have had bad feelings about her, someone who was giving her a hard time?"

Ambrose wrinkled his forehead for a split second and said, "I don't remember anything like that. Everyone liked Leslie. She was a ray of sunshine. I can't imagine anyone not liking her."

Claire looked at the man's face and wondered how he managed to reach middle-age without discovering that it is impossible to win everyone over, that on occasion, you might find someone who doesn't care for you. "Did Leslie ever mention someone she had a personality conflict with or someone she'd had an argument with? Anything like that?"

Ambrose wore a sunny smile on his face. "Not once. You didn't know Leslie. You could not help but enjoy her company."

"No conflicts on the dig?" Nicole asked. "Everyone got along well?"

"It was one of the best digs I've ever been on."

"Did you and Leslie keep in touch after leaving Iraq?" Claire questioned.

Ambrose nodded. "Whenever I was in Cambridge, we'd meet for coffee."

"Could you estimate the number of times you got

together? What would you say? Was it once a week? Once a month?"

"Oh, gee, let's see. I'd say once a month, at the most."

Claire once again asked about the young graduate student's mood. "When you got together, did it ever seem like something was bothering Leslie? Was she worried or concerned about anything?"

"Nothing." Ambrose shook his head. "Everything always seemed great. We'd talk about our work, people we knew, things like that. Leslie was always upbeat whenever we got together."

"Leslie died about eight months after the Iraq trip?" Nicole asked.

Ambrose calculated the time in his head. "That's correct."

"So you probably saw her eight or nine times between the time you returned from Iraq and her death?"

"That sounds about right."

"Are you married, Professor Ambrose?"

"Divorced."

"How long have you been divorced?"

Ambrose sat straighter. "I've been married twice. The first marriage lasted about two years. My second wife and I divorced after five years." He smiled and gave a shrug. "I guess I have a hard time choosing a woman who is right for me."

"Do you have kids?" Nicole asked.

"No kids. That's for the best, I suppose."

Claire said, "We saw some pictures of the Iraq dig. There was a photo of an excavation tool. It was a trowel with some inlays of mother-of-pearl in the handle."

Ambrose swallowed hard and blinked a few times.

"Did the trowel belong to you?"

"I had one like that. The tool in the picture might have been mine."

"It looked like a finely-crafted object. Do you still have it?" Nicole asked lightly.

"No, I don't. I don't recall what happened to it. I suppose I misplaced it on a dig."

"Leslie had a trowel like the one you owned," Claire pointed out.

"Did she?" Ambrose averted his eyes and took a swallow from his mug.

Claire asked, "Do you know where she got it?"

"Me? No. How would I know?"

Claire smiled reassuringly. "I thought maybe Leslie admired the one you had in Iraq and bought a similar one for herself. I thought she might have asked you where you purchased the tool."

Ambrose's words came out in a rush. "I don't recall her asking me about it. I don't know. It was a long time ago. Perhaps you're right. She may have liked the one I had so she got one for herself. Why do you ask about it?"

"We wondered if the trowel in Leslie's apartment had once belonged to you."

"No. I didn't give it to her."

"Could it have gotten mixed up with her things and she kept it?"

"Maybe. I don't know. Probably not. I haven't seen that trowel for decades."

"I apologize in advance for my next question," Claire told the man. "I'm sorry if it seems indelicate. Were you and Leslie in a relationship?"

Ambrose's eyes became as wide as saucers. "Absolutely not. We were friends. I was married. I never engaged in a relationship with her."

Nicole lowered her chin and made eye contact with Ambrose. "Did you want to have a relationship with her?"

"No, of course not. We were colleagues. I was married." Ambrose's facial muscles tensed.

Claire said, "Some people we talked with

mentioned that you and Leslie had a flirtatious relationship while on the dig."

The man's cheeks tinted pink. "We got along well. We joked, we talked. I don't think that's being flirtatious." Ambrose raised an eyebrow and shook his head dismissively. "Who came up with that bit of nonsense? And why would they say such a thing?"

"I don't recall who said it," Claire told him.

"It's just not true." Ambrose forced a smile. "Someone has a vivid imagination."

"So you had no interest in Leslie from a relationship standpoint?" Nicole asked.

"None whatsoever. I absolutely did not. I'm baffled by the accusation."

"It wasn't an accusation," Claire gently corrected the professor. "It was only someone's impression."

"Well." Ambrose seemed to want to say more, but he stopped himself.

"Had you ever been to Leslie's apartment?" Nicole used a light tone of voice. "For a get-together or a party?"

"I don't remember ever being there. When we saw each other, it was for a quick cup of coffee."

Claire asked, "Was there anyone that you suspected might be her killer?"

Ambrose's mouth opened in surprise at the bluntness of the question. "I have no idea."

"Did you think it might have been someone she knew or was familiar with?" Claire asked.

"I didn't suspect anyone. I thought it was random. Someone broke in and ...." He let his voice trail off.

"What was the talk at the time? Were people thinking it was a random break-in? Did people think something else had happened?"

"I don't know." Ambrose knuckles turned white as he gripped his mug. "We were waiting for the police to catch the killer. We, at least I, thought it would be solved quickly. I had no idea Leslie's death would remain unsolved for almost thirty-five years after the fact." Ambrose shook his head slowly. "It's appalling, really. Why didn't they catch the person responsible?"

"We'd like to know the answer to that question," Claire said. "That's why we're helping interview people who knew Leslie. Maybe someone will remember some small thing that will lead to more information."

"I hope so."

"What about a friend of Leslie? Did you know any of her friends?"

"No, I didn't. I only met some of her friends at the memorial service and I don't even know what their names were." Ambrose's eyebrow went up. "Leslie was friendly with a young woman on the dig. She lived in the same building in Cambridge as Leslie. Amy Wonder. Have you talked to her?"

"We haven't yet, but we have plans to," Claire said. "What did you think of Amy?"

"She was great. A nice person. Quieter than Leslie, but easy to talk to, serious about her work, smart, friendly. As I said, everyone worked well together."

"Leslie and Amy got along well? No arguments? No disagreements?"

"None that I knew about. They appeared to be good friends."

"Did Leslie talk about any other of her friends?"

"No. Our conversations centered around our work, the dig, people who worked in Iraq with us. We didn't socialize together so we didn't know many people in common."

"Did you know Leslie's boyfriend, Peter Safer?"

"I didn't know him. I don't believe we ever met."

"Did Leslie talk about him?"

"Not much. I knew she had a boyfriend. She must have mentioned him when we were on the dig, but she didn't talk about him very much. At least, not to me."

"Did you get the impression she was serious about Safer?"

Ambrose said with a bit of sarcasm, "I wouldn't have said they were serious since Leslie barely mentioned him. If you're serious about someone, you usually bring them up, say you miss them, talk about the person. No. I didn't think her relationship with him seemed serious at all."

Claire gave a nod. "Is there anyone you can think of who might be helpful for us to talk with?"

Ambrose glanced out of the coffee shop window. "Maybe the other people on the dig? People who lived in her apartment building? Some of the students and staff in her department?" He put his mug on the table. "The police must have talked to all of them already."

"Did the police question you at the time?" Nicole asked.

"No, they didn't. I suppose the dig in Iraq was too far in the past to think any one of us knew anything important."

Claire completely disagreed with that statement. She was sure someone knew something ... and that it was definitely important.

12

Amy Wonder walked out of her office at the Boston museum wearing a blue blazer, white shirt, and a black skirt. In her late fifties, Dr. Wonder was petite and athletic-looking and wore her sandy-colored hair in short layers around her face. She welcomed Claire with a smile and a firm handshake.

"Very nice to meet you," Claire said. "My friend, Nicole, couldn't make it so it's just me today."

Amy ushered Claire into her office with a window looking out at the Boston neighborhood, walls of bookshelves, and a neat desk with only a laptop and a leather folder on it.

After offering Claire something to drink, Amy said, "I was surprised to get your email. I hadn't realized it was almost thirty-five years since Leslie was killed." The woman sat in her desk chair swiveled around towards her guest. "And still unsolved."

"We have an associate who recently retired and now plans to spend his time looking into the murder." Claire rested her arms on the sides of her chair as she explained Marty Wyatt's desire to find the killer. "Mr. Wyatt has asked me to help him by talking with people who knew Leslie."

"I see. Is your associate hopeful he can make some headway?"

"He's hopeful, but not naive. You never know when something will turn things around and point investigators in the right direction. All we can do is try."

Amy gave a nod.

"You lived in the same building Leslie did? On the same floor?"

"I did. With my roommate Jill Lansing. Leslie lived across the hall."

"You and Leslie were friends?"

"Not exactly friends. We were friendly. We chatted, had drinks sometimes, got together to watch a movie. Even though we studied in the same department, we had different friends and moved in different circles. Everyone was busy. We weren't always at home at the same time."

"You and Leslie went on a dig in Iraq together?"

"We did. I got to know her better there. We had a great time. It was hot and hard work, but the group was fun and everyone got along really well."

"What was Leslie like?" Claire asked.

"Leslie was funny and smart and loved archaeology. She was fun to be around, upbeat, positive, made the best of everything."

"Someone told me that Leslie and Professor Ambrose seemed close."

Amy tilted her head. "They liked each other, teased each other. They were playful, flirty, but that's all it was. Professor Ambrose was married. Leslie was seeing Peter Safer. Leslie and Ambrose weren't in a relationship. If that's what the person meant, he or she was mistaken."

"Was Leslie serious about Peter?"

"I'm not sure. They were often on again, off again." Amy shrugged. "We were young."

Claire asked softly, "Can you tell me about the night of the murder?"

Amy's lip seemed to quiver for a second. "I was in my apartment with Jill and my boyfriend, Henry. Our door was open. We always kept it open when we were at home. Leslie and her boyfriend, Peter, came by. They'd been out for pizza. We talked for a while and then Peter left. Leslie stayed a little longer and then went back to her apartment." Amy looked down at her hands. "That was the last time I saw Leslie alive."

"Did you stay up late?"

"Jill left to go to her boyfriend's place. Henry went to his apartment down the hall about forty-five minutes after Leslie left my apartment. I went to bed about thirty minutes later. I read in bed for a little while, but I couldn't keep my eyes open so I turned off the light."

"Did anything wake you?"

"You mean did I hear anything?" Amy seemed to stiffen. "I didn't hear a thing. I slept all night." Letting out a slight sigh of annoyance, she said, "The police asked me over and over again. Did you hear anything? Why didn't you hear anything? What kind of a question is that? I didn't hear anything because I didn't hear anything." Amy looked at Claire. "They kept badgering me about it, like I was lying about hearing nothing. They made me feel guilty that Leslie was killed and I was just sleeping in my bed in the next apartment. It almost seemed they wanted me to make something up, tell them I *did* hear a scuffle or a shout."

"Did Leslie keep her door open when she was at home?"

"She didn't, but the door was always unlocked. The lock was difficult. It would never lock when she turned the key so she basically never bothered."

Claire said, "You were awake for only about an hour after Leslie left your room that night. She had an exam the next day. She may have stayed up late studying. She could have been awake when the intruder entered her room."

"It's possible."

"But, if she was awake, wouldn't she have screamed or cried out when the attacker showed up?"

"I would think so," Amy said. "But the person could have sneaked in quietly and surprised her. He could have hit her before she knew he was there."

Claire said, "And if she was asleep, she was probably attacked before she could wake up. In either case, it would answer the question of why no one heard her scream."

"That's right." Amy seemed relieved that Claire wasn't blaming her for not hearing Leslie in distress.

"There's another scenario," Claire said.

Amy's face took on a worried expression.

"The attacker was someone Leslie knew. She wasn't alarmed when the person showed up. Maybe he or she talked in her room with Leslie sitting on the bed. Leslie could have looked down and at that moment, the assailant attacked so quickly, Leslie didn't have a chance to cry out."

"That works, too." Amy nodded.

"Which do you think it was? Someone she knew or someone random?" Claire watched the woman's face.

"I really don't know what to think."

Claire waited a couple of seconds and then asked, "You and Peter went into the apartment the next day? You found the body?"

Amy's face seemed to pale and her eyes shifted around the small office. "Peter arrived and went into the apartment. He found Leslie on the bed. He came to my door and pounded on it. He shouted my name ... he called for Jill. Jill wasn't at home ... she was still at her boyfriend's. I couldn't imagine what was wrong with him. I was studying and had the door shut. I rushed and flung it open. I'll never forget the look on Peter's face." Amy clutched her hands together. "Peter grabbed my arm. His voice was high and it cracked when he said her name. He kept saying, Leslie, Leslie, over and over." The woman swallowed. "I asked him what was wrong. He was scaring me. He finally said that Leslie was dead. I almost had a heart attack. Honestly, for a moment, it felt like my heart stopped."

"You went with him to the apartment?" Claire asked softly.

"He tugged on me. I followed him. Leslie's door was open. Peter must have left it open when he ran from the place. We went inside. I was walking so slowly. My heart was pounding. When we got to the threshold of the bedroom, Peter stepped to the side and started to sob. I inched into the room. I was sure I was going to faint." Amy took in a long, slow breath. "Leslie was on the bed, on her back. There were things on top of her, some blankets, a coat. I tip-toed to the bed and whispered her name. I couldn't believe she was dead. For a stupid second, I wondered if Leslie and Peter were playing an awful joke on me. If it was a joke, Peter should have won an Oscar for his performance. I reached out and lifted the coat from her face." Amy's voice hitched. "There was so much blood."

Neither woman said a word while Amy collected herself. "I haven't thought about all of this for a long, long time. It's something I tried very hard to forget."

Claire waited a little longer and then asked, "I read something about red powder in the room. There was red powder sprinkled around the scene?"

"I didn't even notice it at first. I was so shocked by what had happened. My mind couldn't process it. I only noticed the powder when we came back to the room with Henry Prior. I was so stunned that Leslie was dead that I wasn't thinking straight. I grabbed Peter's arm and pulled him out of there and down the hall to Henry's apartment. We got Henry and went back to Leslie's room. He took one look at her and ran to his place to call the police. Peter went with him. I stood there in the room ... just staring at the bed, at Leslie buried under the coat and blankets. It was like time stopped. My eyes wandered around the room. I noticed the red powder and wondered what in the world it was."

Amy took a deep breath. "Henry came back after he called the police. He took my arm and walked me to the living room where we waited. Peter was in the hall sitting on the floor, slumped against the wall." The woman touched her forehead. "I felt like I was in some alternate universe or something. I felt like I'd left my body and was hovering over the scene watching."

"Was the red powder on the body?"

"Yes, it was. I saw it on Leslie when I lifted up the coat."

"What about the window?" Claire asked.

"The window?" Amy blinked not comprehending.

"In Leslie's room. Was it open?"

Amy looked out the window of her office for several moments. "The police asked me the same question. I'm not sure."

"Think about entering the room. The windows were on the left wall. Leslie liked to sleep with the windows open." Claire kept her voice calm and encouraging. "What sort of day was it? Was it hot? Cooler?"

"It wasn't hot. It was cooler than it had been. The few days before had been too hot, our apartments were steamy, but then it cooled down the day before Leslie died."

"How did it feel in her apartment? Can you remember walking into the place? Was it uncomfortably warm?"

Amy turned her head slowly to Claire, her eyes wide. "When I was in the bedroom alone with Leslie's body ... when Henry and Peter went to call the police ... I remember looking around the room. I saw the red powder. Leslie was on the bed. It felt stuffy in there. The window, it was only open about an inch. I thought about opening it wide, but I couldn't move my legs."

Claire nodded. "When you were in the bedroom, did you happen to notice Leslie's excavation tools? She kept some of them in a wooden box."

"I'd seen the box. It was usually on the bookcase in the living room."

"Did you see it that day?"

"I don't think so. I didn't pay attention. It was probably there, but I don't recall seeing it."

"Were there any tools in the bedroom?" Claire asked.

"I'm not aware of any. There could have been."

"The murder weapon has never been found," Claire said. "Did you notice anything on the bed? A tool? A hammer? A rock? Anything that might have been used as a weapon?"

"I only lifted the edge of the coat that was covering Leslie. I didn't see anything on the bed."

Claire gave the woman a soft smile. "Leslie had a trowel she used on digs. It had mother-of pearl inlays in the handle. Did you ever see it?"

"Yes. It used to be Professor Ambrose's. He gave it to Leslie when we were in Iraq."

"Professor Ambrose gave it to her?" Claire's heart began to pound.

"Leslie liked it," Amy said. "She asked where he got it. I saw it in her tool box when we were leaving Iraq. Leslie told me Professor Ambrose gave it to her."

A shiver ran over Claire's skin. When she and Nicole talked with Professor Ambrose, he had conveniently left that fact out.

13

Dr. Henry Prior, now in his sixties, was a medical anthropologist working as a researcher at one of the larger Boston hospitals. Claire arrived at his office in the hospital to find a medium-height, medium-weight, slightly balding man with clear blues eyes. Prior met Claire with a warm smile and a firm handshake and he ushered her into his ninth-floor office with huge windows looking over the city.

"I'm very pleased that you're looking into Leslie's death. I can't believe it's been almost thirty-five years since it happened." Prior removed his glasses, cleaned them with a small cloth, and placed them back on his head. He looked at Claire with a sigh. "How can I help?"

"I'd like to get your impressions from the time of the murder. I'd like to know more about Leslie Baker. Anything you can tell me will be helpful."

"Where should I start?" Dr. Prior asked.

"You were a student in the anthropology department?" Claire asked.

"I was. As you know, my specialty is medical anthropology."

"And you lived in the same building with Leslie?"

The man gave a slight nod. "Our apartments were on the same floor. Leslie was a second year student then. I was a sixth year, working to finish up my dissertation."

"You were dating Amy Wonder at the time?" Claire asked.

"Yes, we'd been dating for about two years."

"You broke off the relationship?"

"We did. We both felt it wasn't the right match. The breakup was mutual with no hard feelings between us."

"Did you grow apart, is that what happened?"

"None of us who knew Leslie were in very great shape, probably for a year after it happened. I think Amy and I weren't that supportive of each other. When something like that hits close to home, you have to struggle your way through feelings of grief and horror." Prior paused for a moment. "The world doesn't feel safe anymore. You're not as resilient as you once might have been. Little things bother you. You're not as patient. Your feelings are raw. Amy's and my relationship suffered from having to deal with Leslie's murder."

"Can you tell me a little about Leslie?"

Prior smiled. "She was a lot of fun. Witty, intelligent, a great conversationalist, always ready for an adventure. She took her work seriously. Leslie loved her chosen field, loved going on digs. She knew a lot about different subjects, was well-read, knew current events."

"That was Leslie's first year living in the building?"

"Yes, it was. Her first year, she lived in the graduate dorms."

"Did you know her before she moved into the building?"

"I might have seen her around, but we had never been introduced. She was at the beginning of her studies, I was at the end so we didn't really cross paths much."

"Did you socialize with one another?"

"Sometimes we did. Amy and Jill lived in the apartment across from Leslie. I was down the hall, near the front of the building. There was another person across from me. Amy, Jill, Leslie, me, sometimes Peter, would get together to watch a movie, talk, have a few drinks, play cards. We usually congregated in Amy and Jill's place. It had a bigger living room."

"How did everyone get along?"

"Great. We enjoyed each other's company."

"Before the murder, did Leslie seem out of sorts, angry or upset about anything?"

Prior's face took on a serious expression as he thought back over the decades. "I can't say I picked up on anything. I don't recall Leslie seeming different. She didn't tell me about anything that was upsetting her. She might have confided in Amy or Jill though."

"On the morning after the murder, Amy and Peter came to get you?"

Prior stiffened as he moved his gaze to the top of his desk. When he spoke, his voice was soft. "They did. It was around noon. I'd slept late and was eating breakfast when they came to my apartment. Peter shouted my name from the hall. My door wasn't locked ... they barged right in. As soon as I saw their faces, I knew something was very wrong."

Letting out a long breath, he went on with the

story. "They were babbling and I could barely understand what they were saying. All I could make out was that something was wrong with Leslie. We hurried back to Leslie's place and went into the bedroom. As soon as I stepped into the room, I knew it was bad. Leslie was on the bed. She was covered with a blanket, a coat, some other things. It looked ridiculous, all these items piled up on her. Amy told me to pull the blanket back." Prior's hands balled up. "I knew she was dead. There was blood, on her face, neck, around her head. It took a very long time not to see that scene over and over in my dreams."

"Did you notice anything that might have been the murder weapon?"

"I didn't, no."

"What happened next?" Claire questioned.

"I turned around and went back to my apartment. I called the police."

"Why didn't you call from Leslie's apartment?"

Prior brought his hand to his temple. "I don't know why. Maybe subconsciously I just wanted to get out of there. I didn't even think of using Leslie's phone."

"After you called, did you return to Leslie's place?"

"Yes. I went back. Peter was sitting in the hallway

outside Leslie's apartment. He was leaning against the wall, he had his head in his hands. Amy was still in Leslie's bedroom, just standing there where we left her. I took her hand and we went to the living room, sat on the couch and waited for the police. Amy broke down in tears. It seemed to take so long for the cops to arrive."

Claire waited a few moments before asking, "No one heard shouts or screams or noise of a struggle that night?"

Dr. Prior shook his head. "I didn't hear anything. No one on our floor heard anything."

"When you were in Leslie's bedroom, did you notice if the window was open or closed?"

"I think it was closed, but I wasn't paying any attention to the windows. I can't say for sure."

"Do you think someone might have come in through the window? Do you think it was a random murder?"

"No, I don't." Prior's voice was strong. "I never believed it was a random thing. The front door of the building was always unlocked. Wouldn't someone who wanted to get in try the door first? Wouldn't a person climbing up the fire escape be suspect? Why call attention to yourself like that? It was late at night. Just walk in the front door."

"That makes sense," Claire said. "So was it a random person who came in the front door or was it someone Leslie knew?"

"It was someone Leslie knew." Prior nodded to emphasize his words. "Otherwise, wouldn't she have cried out?"

"She might have been asleep when the intruder came in." Claire watched Prior's face.

"I don't think so. The police put the time of death at around two hours after we were all together in Amy's apartment. Leslie came home from being out with Peter and she stopped by to chat. After about forty-five minutes, Leslie went home and then Jill left for her boyfriend's place. I left about an hour after Leslie. In my apartment, I had a beer and went to bed. I couldn't have been in a very deep sleep when the intruder committed the crime. I think Leslie might have stayed up for a while to study. When I left Amy's apartment, I saw light under Leslie's door. By the time she went to bed, she couldn't have been in a very deep sleep when the killer arrived. If she'd just dozed off, she would have heard him."

"So you think someone Leslie knew came by and she let him in?"

"I think so, yes."

"If they'd gotten into a fight, wouldn't someone on the floor have heard them yelling?"

"Maybe they didn't yell. Maybe they had words and the killer became furious and struck out at her. It might have been quick."

"Do you think it was premeditated?"

"Possibly."

"Had you ever seen red powder in Leslie's apartment?"

"No. I don't know what that was about. Leslie may have had it in her place for painting. Just because I never saw it, doesn't mean it wasn't there."

"Do you remember seeing the red powder in the bedroom that morning?"

Prior blinked. "I don't know. Honestly, I don't know if I noticed it or thought it was blood spatter or maybe I think I saw it because I've heard others talk about it. I was in shock. I don't know if what I remember about that day was how it was or how I think it was."

"It's a very honest answer." Claire made eye contact with the man. "Did the police ask you all of these questions? Did they talk to you more than once?"

"They talked to me the day we found Leslie. I

also went into the station one day to answer more questions."

"Do you think they considered you a suspect?"

Prior looked surprised at the question. "They might have initially. They seemed satisfied with my answers. They talked to me only the two times."

"When you think back on that night, do you recall if you slept well?"

Prior's jaw seemed to slacken. "I remember having a restless sleep. I think it was because I had too many beers that night. I didn't drink a lot, but they seemed to hit me hard. I was wound up about my dissertation. I'd had a meeting with my advisor and he was hard on me. I was upset about it."

"You tossed and turned?"

"I woke up after falling asleep. I couldn't fall back so I got up and had a glass of milk."

"Did you notice the time when you woke up?"

"I didn't."

Something about what Prior had said picked at Claire. "When you were awake, did you hear anyone talking in the hallway, anyone walking out in the hall or on the stairs?"

"No. I got the glass of milk and went back to my room. I didn't hear anyone in the hall."

"Did you go right back to sleep?"

"I sat in the chair by my window and drank the milk, then I went to the bathroom and got back in bed." Prior's eyebrow went up. "My bedroom is at the front of the building, almost right over the front door. While I was in the chair, I heard the door thud closed and I leaned to look out. It was only Peter. He was leaving the building."

"Peter Safer? Leslie's boyfriend?"

"Yes. He must have been studying with Leslie."

"If that was the case, then the murder must have been committed after Peter left the building and you went back to sleep?"

"Yes, it must have been. I fell into a deep sleep after I had the milk and didn't wake up until 11:30 the next morning."

Claire kept her voice even when she made her next comment. "You didn't mention that Peter was in Amy's apartment when you were all together the night of the murder."

"Didn't I?" Prior's forehead scrunched. "I think he was there. I'm pretty sure he was. Yes, he left Amy's before I did. He must have come back to study with Leslie."

"And you didn't take a look at the clock when you woke up during the night? Can you make a guess what time it was?"

"I didn't look at the clock. I have terrible eyesight, but I didn't have my glasses on. I didn't bother to look at the clock because I wouldn't have been able to see it."

"But you were able to see Peter Safer leaving the building that night?"

"Peter was under the light that was over the building's front door. People have a distinctive way of moving. I could tell it was Peter."

"Did you tell the police you saw Peter leaving the building late at night?"

"I must have."

Claire gave a nod, but something about Dr. Prior's information didn't sit right with her. *Why didn't it?*

14

Claire entered Tony's Market to see Tony and Tessa flirting with one another across the counter like two teenagers. Tessa's bright smile remained on her face when she saw Claire, but Tony erased his grin, pulled himself up to full height, and adjusted his white apron while his cheeks turned pink. The Corgis ran over to Tony with wagging tails.

"Afternoon, Blondie." He nodded to the woman standing on the other side of the counter from him before bending down to pat his two favorite dogs. "Tessa's here."

Claire tried to stifle a chuckle. "I can see that." She went to Tessa and gave her a hug.

"How are things going?" Tessa eyed the young woman. "Is everything okay?"

"Yes." Claire and Tessa headed to the small café table at the back of the store where Augustus Gunther sat with his newspaper and a cup of coffee. The women greeted the older judge and sat down with him.

Claire said, "Nicole and I have been interviewing people about the Leslie Baker cold case. I get the feeling some of them are not telling us the full story."

"Maybe it's the full story as they know it," Tessa suggested.

"Or as they remember it," Augustus added. "It was a long time ago. Things have a way of getting embellished or changed or deleted."

"So some might not be intentionally trying to mislead us?"

"I'd say that probably is correct." Augustus lifted his mug.

Narrowing her eyes, Claire said, "But others *might* be trying to mislead."

"It's possible." Augustus adjusted his bow tie. "Why would someone do that?" the man asked as if he were instructing a law school class.

"Because," Claire said. "The person might know

the killer and is protecting him ... or the person giving me wrong information might be the killer himself."

"Any other reasons to mislead?"

Claire tilted her head to the side in thought. "I can't think of any."

Augustus proposed an idea. "Perhaps, the person you're talking to has a gripe against someone and wishes to present some evidence to make that someone a suspect."

Tessa looked questioningly at the judge. "Why wait until now to make a false claim against someone? Why not tell the police right away?"

Augustus raised an eyebrow. "Maybe the person did tell the police. Maybe it went nowhere and the person is now trying again."

"That's too complicated." Claire sighed, stood up and went to the coffee and tea bar to pour herself and Tessa cups of tea. When she sat down in her chair, she said, "My head is spinning from talking to these people. Professor Ambrose claimed he did not give his trowel to Leslie, but Dr. Amy Wonder told me matter-of-factly that Professor Ambrose gave the trowel to Leslie in Iraq because Leslie admired the object."

"One of them doesn't remember correctly." Tessa sipped the hot liquid.

"Dr. Wonder thinks the window in Leslie's bedroom was open a crack, but Dr. Henry Prior doesn't think it was." Claire leaned forward. "Dr. Prior told me he woke up shortly after he fell asleep and saw Peter Safer leaving the building, but when I asked if Peter had come up with Leslie after their date and visited in Amy Wonder's apartment, he told me he wasn't sure, *maybe* Peter was there."

Tessa asked, "Did anyone report that Peter was with Leslie in the building that night?"

"Marty's notes say that Peter dropped Leslie off after the date and then he went home. It doesn't say he went into the building with her." Claire rubbed at the muscle tension in her neck. "Peter told me he went inside with Leslie and went to Leslie's apartment to help unstick the bedroom window. Then he claims he left to go home. Amy said that Leslie came to her place and they talked for a while."

"So Peter wasn't at Amy's place?" Tessa asked.

"Dr. Prior was the only one who said he didn't remember if Peter was there or not. Peter and Amy say he wasn't there."

Augustus stroked his chin. "Henry Prior reported

seeing Mr. Safer leaving the building late at night, supposedly after Peter had already headed home."

"That's right," Claire nodded.

Augustus asked, "Could Prior be mistaken? Could Prior have been awakened by noise in Leslie's apartment? Maybe there was a struggle and Prior woke from the sounds. The murder had been committed by the time he was fully awake and got out of bed to go to the kitchen for a glass of milk. When Prior returned to his bedroom and looked out of his window, he saw someone leaving the building. It could have been Leslie's killer."

"Yes," Claire said. "All of that is plausible. Dr. Prior may not have realized he woke up from noise of a struggle in Leslie's room."

"So you're surmising the killer is Peter Safer?" Tessa looked at Augustus.

"Not at all. It may have been Mr. Safer, it may have been the killer making his escape, or it may have been someone else just leaving the building." Augustus's blue eyes clouded. "Or, Dr. Prior is lying about seeing someone outside."

Claire sat up straight. "Why would he do that?"

"Perhaps, Dr. Prior would like to pin the murder on Peter Safer."

"Why would he want to do that?" Claire's eyes were wide.

"Could Dr. Prior be the killer?" Augustus speculated.

Claire's mouth opened a little. "So Prior tries to shift attention to Peter Safer and away from himself."

"Why would Dr. Prior kill Leslie?" Tessa questioned.

Claire shook her head as she shrugged a shoulder. "Could they have been seeing each other and had a terrible fight?"

"If Leslie and Henry Prior had been seeing each other, it brings up another possibility," Augustus said.

Tessa and Claire stared at the man.

"At the time Leslie was killed, Prior and *Amy Wonder* were in a relationship with one another."

Claire's lips tightened into a thin line. "You're suggesting that Leslie and Henry Prior may have been involved with one another and Amy Wonder found out about the affair and killed Leslie?"

"Nothing can be disregarded, can it?" Augustus asked.

"What a tangled web." Tessa shook her head.

"None of this feels right." Claire rested her chin in her hand. "I'm missing something."

Augustus folded his newspaper and drained his coffee before standing up. "I'm off to meet a friend." He addressed Claire. "Keep your mind open. You'll find what you're missing. You always do." The judge headed to the front of the store, said a few words to Tony, and stepped out of the market into the September sunshine.

"Augustus always makes me think and rethink," Claire said.

Tessa glanced over her shoulder to see where Tony was in the store. She kept her voice low. "Have you sensed any danger when you've been talking to these people about the young woman's murder?"

A shiver of anxiety ran down Claire's back. "I haven't. I've felt that some aren't fully telling me what they know and I question some people's motivations and suspicions, but I haven't felt in any danger."

"I don't like this case." Tessa ran her hand over her arm. "Stay on your toes, Claire. Question everything."

"I will." Wanting to lighten the dark mood she was feeling, Claire changed the topic of discussion with a gleam in her eye. "In fact, I'm now going to question you about Tony."

Tessa blushed and sat back in her seat. "He's a very nice man."

Claire leaned forward with a conspiratorial grin. "Have you two been seeing each other?"

"From time to time." Tessa picked up her cup and sipped.

"From time to time? What does that mean?" Claire pressed. "Once a month? Once a week?" She gave Tessa a wide smile and narrowed her eyes. "Once a day?"

Tessa leaned back and let out a hearty laugh causing Tony to call back to them. "What's so funny back there?"

Claire teased, "We're talking about you."

Tony let out a grunt. "Bah."

"Well?" Making eye contact with Tessa, Claire tapped the tabletop. "You didn't answer my question."

Tessa looked away from Claire. "I haven't been keeping track of how often I get together with Tony."

"That means you're seeing a lot of each other."

A little smile started at the corner of Tessa's mouth, but she didn't let it spread across her face. "What's the definition of *a lot*?"

Claire folded her arms on the table and leaned closer, her eyes bright. "You like each other."

Tessa met Claire's eyes with a gleam in her own. "Yes, we do."

"That makes me happy. I love Tony like a father. I think he's been lonely." Claire touched Tessa's arm. "I want him to be happy."

"Me, too." Tessa patted Claire's hand. "And what about you and Ian?"

Claire smiled. "I want him to be happy, too."

"I hope the two of you are doing other things together besides running, biking, and swimming." Tessa did not care for exercise and often teasingly asked Claire and Ian why on earth they had any desire to take part in athletic competitions.

"You'll be happy to know that we've been out to dinner, gone to movies, and seen a couple of plays together."

"Thank the heavens," Tessa said with a grin. "I wondered if there was something wrong with you two."

Tony came to sit with the women and Claire brought him up-to-date on what she'd learned about the cold case. After Tony clucked at her to be careful and Claire promised to be on guard, she collected the dogs from the little grassy, fenced-in area behind the market and headed home.

Walking up the short hill to her townhouse, Claire considered two choices for the evening meal and because Nicole was coming for dinner, she decided on her friend's favorite of vegetable macaroni and cheese with salad and fresh rolls. Claire wanted to go for a short run before starting dinner and was calculating the time in her head to be sure it wouldn't make the meal late when Bear and Lady stopped in their tracks in front of the townhouse and whined, refusing to advance.

Claire was so engrossed in her thoughts that she almost stepped on the dogs and had to quickly sidestep to avoid bumping into them. "What's up, you two? What's the matter?"

When Lady whined and looked up at Claire, the young woman crouched to reassure the Corgi and then noticed a spot of something on the second step leading to her front door. Leaning closer to see what it was, she saw another smear of dark red on the next step. Claire's heart pounded. She stood and walked up to the small front landing to see smears of red all over the cement and granite. Anger flooded her veins as she touched one of the streaks with her finger.

Red dust. Ochre. Just like the powder sprinkled over Leslie Baker's dead body thirty-three years ago.

An icy shiver ran over Claire's skin.

15

Claire made a phone call to Ian and he was at her townhouse within ten minutes pulling up to the curb and jumping out with concern etched on his face. Putting his arm around Claire and pulling her close, he asked, "Are you okay? Is there any sign of forced entry?"

Claire was still steaming over someone's attempt at intimidation with the red powder spread over her entryway. "It doesn't look like it. The front door is closed and locked. I didn't walk around to the back so I'm not sure if anyone broke in that way."

A squad car arrived and the officers checked around the building. Samples of the dust were taken and in thirty minutes, the cops were gone leaving Ian, Claire, and the dogs in the townhouse kitchen.

"Who did it?" Claire ranted. "Oh, how I wish there were security cameras out front. How dare someone leave ochre on my steps. How dare someone attempt to harass me."

Ian sat at the kitchen island sipping a coffee. "Have you considered that the person who did this is Leslie's killer?"

Claire stopped pacing around the room and took a deep breath. "I guess, subconsciously, yes." A look of worry washed over her. "I was so angry about someone coming here to try and frighten me there wasn't any room for fear or worry in my head. Until now." She sat on the stool next to Ian.

"I didn't say it to scare you." Ian reached for Claire's hand. "It's just that I don't think it was done as a practical joke. It was done by someone who knows the circumstances of Leslie's death, which wouldn't be hard to know since the detail about the red powder was in the news article the other day." The detective paused. "It was also done by someone who knows you're interviewing people and looking into the case ... and that's the part that worries me."

"Someone's sending me a message." Claire's voice was heavy.

"It might be someone you've talked to already,

but it might also be someone who has heard you're interviewing people related to the death."

"Right. It could be someone I've yet to speak with, but who is in contact with one of the people I've met." Claire crossed her arms on the counter. "That doesn't exactly narrow it down."

"The powder wasn't on the steps when you left this morning?" Ian asked.

"I'm sure it wasn't. When the dogs and I left the house, the steps were clear."

"Then it was done sometime during the day. In broad daylight." Ian looked at Claire. "Bold, isn't it? To do that with no darkness to hide in and when people are walking around the neighborhood. Interesting. Why wouldn't the person spread the powder at night?"

"It wouldn't take long to sprinkle it around," Claire said. "The person could have acted like a tourist. Carry a camera, act like you're interested in the historic buildings, wander around, and when no one is in sight, go up to the door and spread the ochre. What would it take? Five seconds? Not even."

"A neighbor could have been watching out a window though." Ian gestured to the front of the house. "From the other side of the street. There are lots of windows in all these townhouses. A delivery truck could have pulled up. The powder-spreader would have no way of knowing if someone was watching him. It's risky behavior."

Claire said, "He probably had on sunglasses and a hat and kept his head down. He spread the powder and walked away. No one would be able to identify him." She balled her hand into a fist and groaned, saying for a second time, "I wish there was a security camera out front."

Ian's phone buzzed and after glancing at it, he told Claire he had to get to a meeting at the police station. At the front door, he kissed her and held her tight. "Call me anytime. Day or night. I'll be here in minutes."

"I will." Claire smiled warmly at Ian while the Corgis danced around their legs.

"Keep the door locked," Ian said as he walked down the steps to his car. "Don't let anyone in."

"How about me? Can she let me in?" Carrying a pastry box, Nicole crossed the street behind Ian's car and walked towards the townhouse.

Ian took a quick look at Nicole before getting into the driver's seat. "No, she definitely should not let you in," he said and then smiled. "Claire will bring you up-to-date on the latest. Be careful."

Nicole made a face and climbed up the steps to

stand next to Claire. "Why is Ian telling me to be careful?" Noticing the red powder, she asked nonchalantly, "What's this red stuff on the steps?" As soon as the words were out of the brunette's mouth, her face hardened and she turned slowly to her friend. "Is it what I think it is?"

"Yup, it sure is." Claire stepped back so Nicole could enter and before shutting the door, she took quick glances up and down the cobblestone street, her heart beating hard against her chest. "I haven't made any dinner for us."

"That's what phones are for." Nicole headed for the kitchen and put the pastry box into the refrigerator. "What shall we order? Pizza? Thai? Something from the Italian place?"

When the dinner order was placed for delivery, Claire and Nicole carried drinks and cheese and crackers out to the patio where they sat at the table under the shade tree while the dogs lolled in the grass.

"Tell me what's going on," Nicole said.

Claire gave her the rundown on the latest development.

"Who did it?" Nicole's eyes narrowed. "And in broad daylight."

"Ian said the very same thing," Claire told her

friend. “He thinks it was a bold move to sprinkle the powder over the steps during the day. He’ll go around the neighborhood and ask if anyone saw what was happening.”

“Good idea.” Nicole placed a square of cheddar cheese on a cracker. “So what do you think? Is it someone you or both of us have interviewed?”

“I don’t know.” Claire raised her hands in a helpless gesture.

“What about Peter Safer?” Nicole bit into her cracker. “He seemed sort of arrogant and distant, almost annoyed that we had the nerve to question him about the murder.”

“It’s true.” Claire gave a nod. “And Henry Prior said he saw Safer leaving the apartment building *after* Peter claimed he left Leslie.”

Nicole said, “But Henry Prior has bad eyesight and he told you he didn’t have his glasses on the night he saw Safer exiting through the front door. Can his identification of Safer be trusted?”

“I doubt it would hold up in court.” Claire added some wine to Nicole’s glass. “What about Professor Ambrose? He told us he didn’t give Leslie the trowel, but Amy Wonder said Leslie told her Ambrose gave her the trowel as a gift.”

"Too many conflicting stories," Nicole groaned.

Claire swirled the wine in her glass absent-mindedly. "My mind keeps going back to Rosalind Fenwick when she showed up at the chocolate shop with the pictures from the Iraq dig."

"What about it?" Nicole asked.

"Why didn't she tell the police of her suspicion that Leslie and Ambrose were in a relationship? Why didn't she bring up the trowel with the police? The investigators never asked her to talk with them, but she kept silent and kept her thoughts to herself."

"Maybe she didn't think those things would make a difference to the case?" Nicole guessed. "She was young back then. Maybe she assumed the police knew what they were doing and felt awkward about butting into the case."

"But now she comes forward so many years later?"

I don't know." Nicole leaned back in her chair and gave a shrug. "It's probably been bugging her for decades and when she read about Marty looking into the cold case she probably decided to tell what she knows."

"In a way, when Rosalind Fenwick talked to us, she seemed to point the finger at Professor Ambrose.

I think she suspects him, but what she told us didn't seem to add up to very much." Claire watched the dogs resting in the grass. "Does she have more to say or is she deflecting attention away from someone else and onto Ambrose?"

Nicole frowned. "Ambrose didn't help his cause by telling us he didn't give the trowel to Leslie."

"Maybe he *didn't* give it to her. Leslie might have taken it without permission."

"Stole it, you mean?" Nicole shook her head. "Or maybe Amy Wonder is lying that Leslie told her Ambrose gave it to her."

Claire rolled her eyes. "We need to focus on motivation, otherwise we're just going to go round in circles."

"We don't have much to go on. We need to find a reason why someone would want to kill Leslie." Nicole took a swallow from her glass. "Or, we need to find the murder weapon."

Claire gave her friend a smile. "That would be helpful, yes."

"What does your intuition tell you?" Nicole asked.

"Not a heck of a lot." Claire let out a sigh. "I suspect everyone. When we interview someone, I sit there thinking they're lying or they're holding back. I don't trust any of them."

"But that's your mind working. What about your intuition?"

Claire slumped in her chair. "I don't get any strong feelings one way or the other."

Nicole leaned forward over the table. "Next time we interview someone, let me ask the questions and you sit there and listen. Don't focus too much on what the person tells us. Pay more attention to the sensations, the feelings you get from the person. What do you think?"

"Okay. Let's try it."

Nicole beamed. "Who's next on our agenda?"

"This might be good for nothing, but I've set up a meeting with Peter Safer's ex-wife. I thought it couldn't hurt to talk to her. Maybe she can shed some light on Safer, what kind of person he is, what he told her about Leslie, who he might suspect the killer is."

"I think it's brilliant. When do we see her?"

"Tomorrow afternoon."

When the doorbell chimed with the food delivery, both Corgis bounced to their feet and barked. With the dogs rushing ahead, the young women followed them to the front foyer to get the meals and pay the driver.

When Claire opened the door, the person standing there wasn't who she and Nicole expected it to be.

16

Marty Wyatt stood on the front step, his skin looking pasty and gray. Claire was startled to see he had a cane in his hand and was leaning heavily on it. Marty gave them a smile, but it was weak and strained.

"Marty." A hint of surprise sounded in Claire's voice as she moved to take the man's arm and help him into the townhouse.

"I had a late doctor's appointment." Marty's breathing was labored. "I decided to swing by here before going home."

Claire helped him to the living room sofa while Nicole hurried to get the man a cup of tea. With worried expressions on their faces, the young women sat across from him without speaking in order to give Marty a chance to catch his breath.

Wiping a bit of sweat from his brow with a handkerchief, Marty leaned against the soft sofa back. "I'll be okay in a minute. My breathing is shot. Walking is getting tough. Steps? Forget it."

"Was the doctor any help?" Claire asked.

"I'm afraid not." Marty's tone was accepting. "There isn't much they can do for me now except try to make me comfortable." He lifted his head. "I want to thank you both for doing the interviews for me." He rubbed his hands over his thin thighs. "My illness is in a rush to claim me and I'm not going to be able to do anything anymore that takes physical strength."

Claire had to blink fast to push away several tears that tried to gather. "I'm so sorry," she murmured.

"I can work at my laptop to do more research online, but that's about the extent of it." Marty looked from Claire to Nicole. "If you can carry on, I'd be forever grateful, but if it's too much, I certainly understand."

"It's not too much," the women said nearly in unison, their voices sounding thick with emotion over the man's fate.

"I've had a good life and I'm grateful." Marty

stopped to catch his breath. "My only regret is that I didn't do enough to find Leslie's killer."

"You did an enormous amount," Nicole told him. "The police haven't been able to solve it even with all of their resources. You're one person, on your own."

"The information you've gathered is a huge help," Claire said. "When the crime is solved, your sleuthing will be a big part of that success."

Marty rubbed at the side of his face. The brief conversation had tired him and caused his eyelids to droop. "Do you have any suspicions about the people you've talked to so far?"

"We're suspicious of everyone," Claire admitted. She told Marty what they'd learned and what their impressions were of the people they'd talked with.

Marty leaned back against the sofa again and closed his eyes. "I've always thought Professor Ambrose was a butt-kisser, excuse my language. I think he'd say anything to get ahead ... and anything to stay out of trouble."

"Do you think he might be guilty?" Nicole eyed the man.

"I can't say that, but I've kept my eye on him."

"Do you have suspicions about anyone in particular?" Claire watched Marty's face.

"I don't like Peter Safer," Marty said. "He gives

me the idea he's holding back when I've talked to him. I don't like his attitude either. He really doesn't like talking about the murder. Wouldn't you want to do everything you could to find the person who killed your friend?" Marty put his hand on his chest and wheezed for a second.

"I would," said Nicole softly.

"But some people wouldn't." Claire watched Marty closely to be sure he wasn't going into some sort of distress. "People may be afraid of repercussions or reprisals ... or maybe they don't want to stick their noses into it or they can't deal with death and murder so they keep what they know to themselves."

Something about Marty's visit was picking at Claire and her mind worked to figure out why.

The doorbell rang again and Nicole hurried to answer it. "It must be the food. Finally."

Claire said, "We ordered some takeout. There's plenty. Stay and eat with us."

Marty started to protest, but Claire hushed him. "You don't want to have to make dinner when you get home. It would be nice if you join us."

While Nicole prepared three plates, Claire asked Marty if he'd like to go out to the patio table or stay where he was and she'd bring snack trays in for everyone. The man eyed the patio through the sliding glass doors. "The patio sure would be nice."

Taking hold of his arm, Claire managed to get Marty off the couch and when he was steady enough to take some steps, she and Nicole maneuvered him outside and helped him into one of the chairs. Bear and Lady rubbed against the man's leg once he was safely positioned in his seat.

Drinks were brought out and they settled down to eat the lasagna, salad, and garlic bread with Nicole and Claire chattering away about working at the chocolate shop so Marty could listen to the conversation without feeling the need to contribute.

Marty ate slowly taking his time to chew each forkful with care. "Sorry," he apologized. "It takes me a long time to chew." He gave the women a weak smile. "I have to alternate between eating and breathing. Another wonderful aspect of this disease."

"No rush," Nicole patted the man's hand. "Take your time and enjoy it." She winked. "But save room because I brought the dessert."

Marty chuckled and rubbed his tummy. When the three had polished off their meals and coffee and tea were brought out, Nicole carried a platter to the table.

"What do you have there?" Marty's eyes went wide as he stretched to see what was on the dessert tray.

"Nothing elaborate." Nicole set it on the table. "It's apple pie to celebrate the fall season. I know it's not quite fall yet, but the weather is cooler and the apples are in season, so here we are."

"There's whipped cream, too," Claire alerted Marty.

Marty grinned and stared at the pie. "Apple pie is my favorite. I haven't had any in a long, long time. My wife used to make a heck of an apple pie." A flicker of sadness passed over his face. "I can't wait to try it."

After each one of them had two pieces, Marty rated Nicole's pie five stars. "I haven't eaten so well in weeks." Marty's cheeks had a little more color in them and his eyes were brighter and he looked less fatigued.

After some conversation, Claire looked at Marty and said gently, "I've been wondering if you have something to say to us. Even though you weren't feeling well, you made a stop here instead of going right home. Is there something you want to tell us?"

Marty looked down at his empty dessert plate

and passed his hand over his face. "I was feeling pretty down. I was feeling pretty sick. I…."

Claire waited.

"I just wanted to thank the two of you for your help and ask if you'd carry on after I'm gone."

Little zaps of electricity bit at Claire's arms. "Was that all?"

Marty gave a nod, but Claire knew there was more to his visit than that.

"The meal and the pleasant company have revived me. I'm feeling better, but I should get home before the fatigue knocks me down again."

Nicole called a cab for Marty, and while they waited for it to arrive, she and Claire helped the man from the patio into the house and walked with him to the sofa.

Claire told Marty about the red powder she found spread over her steps a few hours ago.

Marty's facial muscles sagged and he stared at Claire with watery eyes. Letting out a curse, he gripped the arm of the couch. "I'm sorry this happened. I never wanted to put either of you in harm's way."

"We agreed to help out of our own free will," Nicole said from the kitchen. "No one forced us."

"She's right," Claire said with a smile. "And anyway, we've been in worse situations."

Marty didn't smile. His face was pinched with worry.

Claire asked, "Have you ever received a message like this? Something that warned you to back off?"

"No, I haven't." Marty's shoulders seemed to give an involuntary shake. "I don't like it. Someone must feel threatened."

"The cab's here." Nicole asked the driver to wait while they assisted Marty from the house.

"I think we should go with you," Claire said. "Make sure you get home okay."

Marty poo-pooed the idea. "I'll be fine." He gave the young women hugs and thanked them for their generosity, and then he patted Bear and Lady on their heads.

Settled in the backseat of the cab, Marty waved goodnight as the vehicle pulled away moving slowly over the narrow, cobblestone road.

Claire and Nicole watched the taxi disappear down the hill and around the corner.

"Poor guy." Nicole wrapped her arms around herself to ward off the chill. "Such a nice man."

Claire let out a sigh. "I got the feeling Marty

came here for a reason other than to thank us and to ask us to keep on with the investigation."

Nicole turned to her friend. "Do you have an idea what the reason might be?"

"I don't, but I think it's important."

"Why wouldn't he tell us then?" Nicole looked puzzled. "Why would he change his mind?"

Claire's shoulders sagged. "Two good questions ... and no answers."

17

As Sandra Wallace, the former Mrs. Peter Safer, walked down the hallway, her heels clicked out a rhythm on the marble floor. A tall, slender woman in her early fifties, Sandra had shoulder-length chestnut hair and was wearing a form-fitting, but tasteful, red sleeveless dress. Ms. Wallace was a vice president of the financial firm and looked every bit the intelligent, efficient, and successful business partner. Extending her hand, she introduced herself with a pleasant smile and led Claire and Nicole to her office. The space had a wall of windows overlooking Boston harbor and was decorated in a modern, understated manner in shades of grays and cranberry.

"I was surprised to get your email," Sandra sat in

a chair next to the sofa grouping of furniture in front of the fireplace. "You understand I, myself, did not know the young woman who was murdered?"

"We know that," Claire said with a slight nod. "We've been talking with a few people who lived on Leslie Baker's floor, a few of her friends, and her former boyfriend ... your ex-husband, Peter. Sometimes people subconsciously hold back in such interviews and we've learned that good information can be gained when we talk to people connected to the interviewees. A little thing that's recalled from a conversation can help a great deal."

"I see. I suppose that makes sense." Sandra crossed her long, lean legs and lightly placed her arms on the sides of the chair. "I haven't spoken with Peter in years though."

"Can you describe Peter for us?" Nicole asked with a smile.

"Peter is an intelligent man, very driven to succeed. Financial security is important to him." Sandra's lips tightened. "It's the number one thing in his life."

"He left his program before completing his Ph.D.," Claire noted.

"He did. I didn't know him then. I met him about

eight years after that. He had his MBA and was working in finance. He didn't mention his doctoral work until we'd been seeing each other for almost a year."

"Did he give a reason why he left academia?" Nicole asked.

Sandra shifted her gaze to the fireplace for a few moments. "His answer was always very simple. He didn't think the life of a professor would be financially rewarding enough."

"Do you think there were any other reasons for the career change?" Claire questioned.

"I think the murder affected him terribly. Peter never talked much about it, but I think, deep-down, he associated the murder with his life doing the doctoral work and probably thought he could chase those awful memories away if he changed his life completely. He was haunted by the crime. He had fitful dreams. I suggested he go for therapy, but he dismissed the idea."

"So he left school and abandoned his plans to teach and do research," Nicole commented.

"I think he loved his field of interest," Sandra said. "But it was all ruined by the murder and he decided he needed to be as far from higher education as he could be." The woman gave a shrug. "So

Peter picked a financially lucrative career that was very different from being an academic."

"Was he happy with his choice?" Nicole asked.

Sandra gave an almost imperceptible sigh. "Peter is never happy. He suffers bouts of depression. He has devoted his life to the accumulation of assets. He has a hole inside of him that he thinks money can fill. It hasn't and it never will."

"Do you think his mood and behavior are a result of Leslie's murder?" Claire asked.

"Most definitely."

"It tainted your marriage?" Nicole asked gently.

"It sure did. I wanted to share my life and good fortune with a partner. Peter was blindly running towards gain, accumulating assets, building his portfolio. No matter how much he amassed, it was never enough. Our relationship didn't make him happy, didn't provide him with contentment." Sandra clasped her hands together and rested them in her lap. "Please know that I loved him ... but I couldn't save him from the damage done to him by that murder."

Claire gave a nod and asked, "Did he ever talk about Leslie?"

"Peter told me they dated, that it was always on-again, off-again. He spoke highly of her," Sandra said. "He described finding her dead body in the apartment. It was heart-breaking and horrible. I know he was never the same person after that. I don't think he ever fully recovered from the trauma."

Remembering that Nicole suggested she sit quietly during the interview in order to better focus on her "sensations" about the person, Claire sat back and listened.

"You never had children?" Nicole questioned.

"Not with Peter. I remarried." Sandra's face lit up. "We have a son and a daughter."

Nicole gave the woman a bright smile and asked several questions about Sandra's family until she moved the questioning back to the ex-husband. "Did Peter mention anyone he suspected of the murder?"

Sandra shook her head. "Peter said the killing was random, that some nut broke in and murdered Leslie. He told me the police will never solve the crime."

"You mentioned you haven't seen Peter in a long time," Nicole said. "Your split wasn't amicable?"

"Peter thought I was betraying him when I asked for a divorce. Honestly, I pity him and I tried to get him help, but he always refused," Sandra said. "I couldn't live with him anymore. I wanted someone who cared for me and showed me affection. I wanted a family." A look of sadness pulled at Sandra's face. "Peter wouldn't speak to me after I approached him about divorce. He didn't challenge or oppose it. It was over quickly."

"Did Peter keep in touch with anyone from his university days?" Nicole asked.

Sandra's eyes went wide. "No, he didn't. He never communicated with any of his friends from the program or with the people he knew socially. He made a clean break. He left that life far behind."

"Did Peter mention anyone he was close to during his studies? A good friend?"

"He was friendly with two people in his department. A young woman, her name was Lucy Flynn, I don't know what year she was, and a man who was a year behind Peter, Scott Rivers. He spoke of them on occasion. I'm not sure what became of them or if they're still in the Boston area."

"Maybe we'll look them up." Nicole made a note of the names on her phone. "Did they know Leslie?"

"I'm not sure," Sandra said.

"Did Peter ever talk about the night of the murder? What he and Leslie did that night? What time he left her apartment?"

"Peter told me they went out for pizza and then had a drink at a pub. He walked Leslie home. He didn't want to stay long because she had an exam the next morning."

"Did he go inside the building? Did he stay for a little while?"

"He said he helped Leslie with her stove ... there was something about it malfunctioning."

"Did he go home after that?"

"He told me he left her place and went home," Sandra said.

"Did he make any stops on his way home?"

Sandra blinked, thinking about the question. "I don't recall."

Nicole asked, "Did he mention returning to Leslie's apartment to study with her that night?"

Sandra's forehead creased in thought. "I don't think so. Why do you ask that?"

"We're only trying to establish a timeline of where and when everyone was that night." Nicole smiled sweetly. "That's all."

A knock sounded on the door and Sandra's assistant poked her head in. "The Collins meeting is about to start." The young woman ducked away as quickly as she'd come.

"I apologize, but I have a meeting." Sandra stood and shook hands with Claire and Nicole. "If there's anything more I can help with, don't hesitate to get in touch." She walked the two visitors to the elevator and said goodbye.

On the way down to the ground floor, Nicole eyed Claire. "What did you think?"

"I think Sandra was sincere and forthcoming. I didn't sense she was hiding anything." Claire watched the floor numbers light up and dim on the indicator panel over the door. "I didn't realize Peter Safer had been so damaged by Leslie's murder. I feel less inclined to be hard on him."

"I hear a *but* in your voice." Nicole stared at Claire.

"But why did Henry Prior say he saw Peter leaving the building long after Peter had supposedly gone home?" Claire turned to her friend. "No one saw Peter return to the building. No one heard people talking in Leslie's room. Did Peter come back to Leslie's apartment or not? It picks at me. Was he there or wasn't he?"

"We could ask him straight out," Nicole said. "We could tell Peter someone saw him leaving the building late at night and ask him for clarification about his whereabouts."

Claire nodded. "Let's see how he reacts ... *if* he'll talk to us again."

The elevator door opened and they stepped out

into the high-ceilinged lobby and headed for the glass doors.

Claire said, "We should look up the two people Sandra said were close to Peter when he was in the doctoral program. We can find out if they're still living around here and if they are, see if they'll talk to us about him."

Stepping out into the sunshine, a thought occurred to Claire and she stopped in her tracks and spun around towards her friend.

"There are four apartments on the floor Leslie lived on," Claire said.

"That's right," Nicole agreed.

"Leslie lived in one, Amy Wonder and Jill Lansing lived in another. Henry Prior lived in the third one. Who was living in the fourth apartment? And why hasn't anyone mentioned that person?"

18

When Claire knocked on the door of Marty Wyatt's spacious condo apartment in Boston's Back Bay, it took a long time for the man to open the door. Marty looked like he'd aged ten years over the past week and a half and he looked almost as bad as he had when he arrived at Claire's townhouse unannounced. He wheezed as he led Claire to the living room where they sat side by side in club chairs facing the large windows looking over Boylston Street.

"We sold our house in Hingham when my wife got sick a few years ago and we moved here to be closer to her doctors, to be near the conveniences of the city," Marty told Claire. "I'm glad I don't have to manage the big house we used to own. Everything is easier for me here."

After some conversation about living in the city, Claire asked the question she came to discuss. "Who lived in the fourth apartment on Leslie's floor? We've talked about everyone else who lived there at the time of the murder, but no one has mentioned who was in the other apartment."

"That apartment turned over at the beginning of the month Leslie was killed. A young man moved in. He was a medical student. He only lived in the building for less than two weeks. He died from a drug overdose a week before Leslie was murdered."

"Oh," Claire said in surprise as little buzzes of anxiety moved through her. "That's terrible. Had he socialized with the others who lived on the floor?"

"They all report that the guy was quiet and didn't seem interested in being friends. He was polite and friendly, but wasn't around much and had been there such a short time, they hadn't gotten to know him."

"What was his name?"

"Allen Day. He was a third year medical student. He moved to Cambridge because his girlfriend lived near Harvard Square and he was starting a rotation at the hospital in the city."

"A drug overdose?" Claire pondered the man's cause of death. "He was a doctor. How would he overdose?"

"Med students have grueling schedules," Marty said. "Some probably turn to drugs to keep them going."

Claire shook her head thinking about the exhausting, stressful training of medical school and how ironic it was to have such an unhealthy environment for people studying for a field designed to manage people's health.

"So the person in apartment four can be crossed off the suspect list," Claire said. "I guess he was never actually on the suspect list since he wasn't alive on the day Leslie was murdered." Shifting in her chair, something about the situation tugged at Claire, but she had no idea why. "This person wasn't friends with Leslie?"

Marty shook his head. "He was rarely around and had lived in the building only a matter of weeks."

"He could have known Leslie before moving in."

"It doesn't seem so," Marty said. "The people on the floor reported that Leslie introduced herself to him when he was moving in."

"Okay, it sounds like there was no previous

connection between Allen Day and Leslie. No one new had moved into the apartment before Leslie was killed?"

"The place was empty. No one had moved in."

Claire looked out the window at the bustling street. "We talked to Peter Safer's ex-wife. She said Leslie's death dealt Peter a terrible blow that she believes permanently changed him. He chases money obsessively, he wasn't affectionate, he has trouble with depression."

"A violent death can shake people to their core. I didn't have a relationship with Leslie and I can't get the murder out of my head. Imagine finding your girlfriend murdered." Marty gave a shudder. "Peter Safer may focus on money because it's something he can control, it's something manageable. That becomes important when things in your life hurtle wildly out of control."

"I can understand that," Claire said softly.

Marty asked, "Who are you going to talk to next?"

Feeling that they weren't making any headway at all on the case, Claire forced herself to sit straighter in her chair and made sure her expression did not give away her negative feelings. "Jill Lansing, Amy's former roommate. She's living in New York, but as luck would have it, she's coming to a conference in Boston in a few days. She's agreed to meet."

"I found Jill easy to talk to. A very pleasant person." Marty let out a sigh. "Unfortunately, nothing she told me was helpful. She's an emergency room doctor now. After she got her Ph.D. she went on to medical school."

"That's a great deal of schooling," Claire said.

"Jill told me she decided to alter the direction of her career after Leslie died." Marty said. "She wanted to be of service to others and she thought she could do more good in medicine than in medical anthropology, so she went on to med school."

Claire shifted around to better face Marty and spoke with a kind tone to her voice. "I don't know how helpful it is to interview these people again. We aren't discovering anything more than when you talked to them. I don't want to give you false hope about how this is going to end."

Marty gave a weak smile. "You know what, Claire? There's no such thing as false hope. I'm one of those crazy souls who believes in miracles. Don't give up. I'm not going to."

Claire reached over, took the man's hand, and held it for a few seconds. "We'll keep plugging along then."

Marty offered Claire coffee and when she accepted, he asked her sheepishly if she would mind making it.

"Of course, I will. You sit and rest."

When Claire returned carrying a tray with coffee mugs, cream, sugar, and some cookies Marty instructed her to find in the kitchen cabinet, she set everything on the small table between the chairs.

"It's not quite the feast you provided me with the other night," he told Claire.

She gave him a smile and said, "You can make dinner for me and Nicole some night when you're feeling better."

"It's a deal." Marty took a swallow of his coffee and cradled the mug in his hands while gazing out the window. "One small thing is all it's going to take to break this case wide open. Maybe we already know the small detail, but we're overlooking it ... or maybe we're not connecting it to the necessary piece."

An uncomfortable tingling sensation ran over Claire's skin. "I think you're right. Why do you think the police didn't give the case the attention it deserved? Why did they seem to bungle so many things?"

"I've spent many hours thinking about that without success."

"Your editor told you to drop your investigation into the case?" Claire asked for clarification.

"He did. The guy was huge. I can still see him sitting behind his desk like an enormous walrus. He didn't like anyone questioning his authority. What he said, was the way it was." Marty gave a slight shrug. "I don't think he was trying to squash the investigation. He just didn't think there was a story there so he wanted me to move on. He didn't give a darn what I thought."

"What about the police officer you were friendly with?" Claire asked. "Didn't he tell you that you should back off the case?"

Marty said, "Again, it wasn't a conspiracy or anything. The cops gave it the attention they thought it required and that was that. My contact in the department was of the mind that you don't keep beating a dead horse, otherwise you get a reputation as a nut or a pain in the butt."

"You don't think they were trying to hide something or protect anyone?" Claire asked.

"I don't think so." Marty let out a sigh. "I don't think the murder was that important to them. A girl got killed. The cops probably chalked it up to a spat with a lover or a boyfriend ... in their minds, no dangerous killer was on the loose."

Claire's eyes flashed. "A *spat*? A young woman is murdered and the cops think of it as a *spat* to dismiss?"

"Times were different back then, Claire." Marty ran his hand over his face. "It bugged the heck out of me. A young woman dead and it seemed that not a lot of effort got put into solving it. The thing has haunted me." He lifted the mug to his lips and sipped. "A cop made an off-hand comment to me that Leslie was probably mixed up in drugs. He was linking her to the overdose death of the medical student on her floor. I think some officers thought she might have been dealing drugs or was mixed up in drugs somehow and got killed because of her associations."

For a few seconds, a wave of dizziness washed over Claire causing her to grasp the arm of her chair. Suddenly, she had a menacing sensation that a dark form was creeping up next to her, but when she whipped her head around, no one was there.

Of course there's no one sneaking up on me, she thought. *What am I thinking?*

Claire tried to get comfortable in her chair, but a feeling of unease made her jumpy.

What am I missing? Drugs? The medical student who overdosed? Was there a connection between Leslie and that student that everyone is overlooking? Claire was sure there was a clue attached to the man who lived in that fourth apartment. *Allen Day*.

"Did you ever interview anyone who knew Allen Day?" Claire asked.

"No, I didn't." Marty looked at Claire quizzically. "Why would I do that? Allen Day was dead when Leslie was killed. Everyone said Leslie and Allen hardly knew each other."

"But, maybe they knew someone in common," Claire said, her mind racing.

Her intuition flashed like a red alert burning in her brain.

19

Claire and Nicole met Dr. Jill Lansing at a coffee shop in the hotel next to the conference center in the Seaport District. Dr. Lansing was a slim, five foot six, with highlighted, dark chin-length hair and blue eyes.

She strode energetically across the hotel lobby and extended her hand. “Call me Jill.”

Inside the coffee shop, they took seats, ordered coffee and tea, and got down to business with Claire and Nicole explaining how they got involved in the case.

“It’s been so long. I was very surprised to hear from you.” Jill added a bit of cream to her coffee. “I’m also very happy to hear that people are still pursuing answers.”

"You weren't in the apartment on the day Peter and Amy found Leslie's body?" Claire asked.

"I was at my boyfriend's place, and really, I'm thankful I wasn't at the apartment. I was spared seeing the terrible scene." Jill looked down for a moment. "It was hard enough hearing about the murder."

"What was Leslie like?" Nicole asked.

"You've probably heard about Leslie from other people you've talked to, and I'll echo what they most likely said. Leslie was full of energy, smart, hard-working, attractive, optimistic, bubbly. She could be the life of the party." Jill paused and took in a breath. "But, I'll tell you a few things you might not have heard. Leslie was also immature in some ways. She loved the attention men gave her. Almost everyone was drawn to her and she ate it up. Sometimes it went to her head."

"How do you mean?" Nicole asked.

"Leslie had an arrogant side. She was the best in many ways, knew it, and flaunted it. I could see her making an enemy. It wasn't like she was mean or didn't care about others, that's not what I'm saying at all. She was caring and kind, but sometimes she let her high spirits get away from her and she could be insufferable ... cocky, high and mighty, a know-it-all.

She was young. I'm telling you this because someone killed her and there might have been things about Leslie that grated on somebody." Jill sat up and leaned forward. "And I am in no way blaming Leslie ... absolutely not. I just mean, if she rubbed an unstable person the wrong way, well, maybe that person, out of jealousy or rage or because of some other irrational reason, did the unspeakable and took Leslie's life." Jill passed her hand over her eyes. "I know it's such a simple, stupid thing to say, but I couldn't believe what happened. I couldn't believe she was gone, her life snuffed out so easily."

"After you completed your doctorate, you went into medicine?" Claire asked.

"I did. When I finished my Ph.D. in medical anthropology, I wanted to use my skills to do something more for people so I decided to apply to medical school. Amazingly, I was accepted and off I went for more schooling." Jill smiled. "My parents thought I was going to be a perpetual student. They were relieved when I finished and actually got a job."

Claire and Nicole chuckled.

"They must be very proud of you," Claire told the woman.

"They're good people. I'm lucky they were my parents. They've always been very supportive. The luck of the draw, I guess. I wouldn't be who I am without them."

"You're an emergency room physician?" Nicole questioned.

"I am. It's a very busy place most days and I get a little bit of everything. Gunshot wounds and knife wounds are a big part of my cases ... car accidents, other kinds of accidents, fights, appendicitis, flu, heart problems. Young, old, and everything in between. I have to be a jack-of-all-trades."

"The way you describe it, it sounds like you're very happy in your career," Claire said.

"I wouldn't want to be doing anything else."

"What did you think of the people who lived on your floor when you were a grad student?" Nicole asked.

"Amy was a good person, easy to live with, a nice person. She had a hard time after Leslie's death ... horrible nightmares, insomnia, some depression and anxiety. She had a hard time focusing which impacted her studies. She and her boyfriend went through a hard time. They eventually broke up. Amy almost dropped out of school, but thankfully, she hung in there."

"Henry Prior was Amy's boyfriend," Nicole said.

"That's right. Henry was studying medical

anthropology, too. He got his doctorate in that specialty."

"You were both in the same field," Claire noted. "It must have been helpful for both of you to have someone close by who was studying in the same area of interest."

Jill gave the two young women a look. "You'd think so, wouldn't you? It wasn't." She set down her mug. "Henry was not a team player. He actually made things difficult for me. Once, I caught him about to take a paper I'd written from my desk. He would put me down in front of professors." Jill shook her head in disgust. "I hid my feelings about Henry from Amy. I acted friendly even though I wanted to wring his neck ninety percent of the time. I was actually thankful when he and Amy broke up."

"How did he get along with the others?" Nicole asked.

"I often wondered if anyone else felt the same as I did. Of course, I would never ask anyone in case I was the only one who thought Henry was a jerk." Jill pulled her chair a little closer to the table. "Honestly? I think Henry had a thing for Leslie. He tried to be a big shot in front of her, but Leslie always shot him down. She could match him, sass for sass, and I don't think Henry liked that one bit. I think he wanted Leslie to fall for him." Jill rolled her eyes. "He was dating Amy, but making eyes at Leslie. I saw him flirting with her more than once."

"Did you mention your concerns to Amy?"

"No way." Jill's eyes widened. "I wasn't getting caught in the middle of that. Amy wasn't dumb. She could see what Henry was doing and he had no clue we knew he had the hots for Leslie."

"How did Henry get along with Peter Safer?" Nicole asked.

Jill said, "Peter was fairly quiet, pleasant, easy-going. Henry loved to challenge the way people thought. He would try to bait Peter into discussions, but Peter never had any of it. He was always calm and handled Henry well. Henry loved to get firey arguments going just for the sake of it. He loved debate, but only when he could win the debate, otherwise he would get sullen and nasty."

"We haven't heard any of this before," Nicole said.

Amy let out a chuckle. "Nobody wants to mention the not-so-great side of people. And no one wants to say anything negative about the dead, gosh no, gloss everything over and make a saint out of the person." She made eye contact with the two young women across from her. "I'd rather remember the person the way they were ... with every one of their bumps and beautiful imperfections, all the shiny good things and the messy not so good things, all wrapped up together to make that person special and unique. Not one of us is perfect, and gosh, how boring the world would be if we were."

"Well said." Claire gave the woman a nod. "We appreciate hearing an unvarnished version of your building-mates."

"I'm telling you how I saw things. Someone else would tell the same thing differently. Maybe with all kinds of information, you'll be able to sort through it and pull out the thing that will solve this long-ago murder."

"Can you tell us about the young medical student who died on your floor from a drug overdose?" Claire asked.

"Right," Jill said. "He overdosed just about two or three weeks before Leslie died. His name was Allen Day. He wasn't around much. I'd chat briefly with him when we ran into each other in the hall."

"Was he friendly?"

"He seemed like a nice person. I only talked to him a handful of times. He was always working or studying. He didn't have the free time the rest of us did. I know first-hand the grind of medical school.

It's all-encompassing. Sometimes, I barely had time to breathe." Jill looked solemn. "And I understand how people are drawn into drugs to keep them going or to dull the stress and anxiety. Allen Day wasn't the first med student to turn to drugs."

"Did anyone on the floor get to know Allen Day?"

"I don't think so. The poor guy didn't have time to socialize." Jill pushed a strand of hair from her eyes. "Once in a while, I'd see Peter at Allen's door chatting with him."

"What about Henry? He was right across the hall from Allen."

"I never saw Henry talking to him that I recall. That doesn't mean he didn't."

"Who found Allen after he passed away?" Nicole asked.

"His girlfriend, poor thing," Jill said. "She hadn't seen him and he wouldn't answer the door or his phone so she called the building superintendent to open the door for a wellness check. I wasn't at home when they found him."

"We've heard rumors that Leslie may have been involved with a Professor Malden Ambrose. Did you know anything about it?"

"I don't know. When Leslie came back from the

Iraq dig, she talked about how great the experience was. I teased her about falling for her professor and she said no, he was married. I don't know if there was anything going on between them or not."

"Do you have a guess about who killed Leslie?"

Jill sighed. "I wish I did. I feel like it must have been someone she knew. I always wondered if it was someone who lived in our building, but why I feel that way, I could never explain."

Claire was beginning to wonder the very same thing.

20

After reading through Marty's notes and doing some internet sleuthing, Claire found the name of Allen Day's former girlfriend in the young medical student's online obituary. At the time of his death, Lucy-Lin Zhou was a fourth year medical student studying at the same university as Allen. Cross-referencing her name, university, and date of graduation to social media outlets, Claire found her on-staff at a hospital in Newton working as an anesthesiologist. Dr. Zhou agreed to meet in the hospital cafeteria and Claire arrived to find a petite, slim woman wearing hospital scrubs, with her black hair pulled up into a loose bun. The doctor greeted Claire with a warm smile.

"I only have a few minutes to eat lunch. Would

you like something? I'll grab a sandwich and we can talk. Have a seat," she pointed to a formica table by the window. "I'll get you a coffee."

The quick, energetic woman was back in a flash and sat down opposite Claire and tore the wrapping off the sandwich. "I apologize for having to wolf this down while we talk."

"Please, eat," Claire said. "I completely understand. Thanks so much for seeing me on such short notice."

"How can I help?" Lucy-Lin dabbed at the side of her mouth with a napkin.

After explaining how she got involved in Leslie Baker's cold case murder, Claire asked about the woman's former boyfriend. "Allen died from a drug overdose?"

Lucy-Lin put her sandwich on the lunch tray. "He did." The doctor rattled off the drugs that were in Allen's body and the effect they'd had on his system. "Allen had an amazing career ahead of him. He was brilliant. But in the case of taking drugs, his common sense was lacking. He did not have the willpower to resist." Lucy-Lin looked down for a moment and shook her head. "For years, I struggled with the feeling I hadn't done enough to warn him off using. I really don't think he would have heeded a warning from anyone. He didn't want to stop. Sadly, if he wasn't internally motivated, there wasn't much we could have done for him. No amount of talking or prodding would have changed the outcome."

"What was Allen like?"

A gentle smile lifted the doctor's lips. "He was handsome, caring, very driven. Allen had a brilliant mind. He would have done so much good for people who needed care. His death can only be described as a terrible, terrible tragedy. Allen would have made important contributions to the field. I'm sure of it."

"How long had you been together?"

"Four years. We met in college. I was two years ahead of him. I applied to med school and came to the Boston area. Allen applied to the same school, was accepted, and joined me in the city."

"He'd just completed his second year?" Claire asked.

"That's right. He was working for the summer at a hospital in Cambridge so he decided to rent the apartment near Harvard Square until the end of August." Lucy-Lin took another bite of her sandwich.

"Allen had only been in the building for about three weeks or so. Had he met some of the people on his floor?"

"I remember he told me he'd met some of them, that they seemed nice, not rowdy. As a med student or intern, it's crucial to be able to sleep when you get the chance. Allen wouldn't be able to tolerate wild parties or really loud music playing on the floor. When he got the time to sleep, that's what he needed to do."

"When I read the reports of Leslie Baker's death, I saw notes about Allen's overdose. Do you know who he bought his drugs from?"

Lucy-Lin said, "Allen found someone near the new apartment. I don't think I knew the person's name. Allen was fully aware that I disapproved of the drugs so he kept things to himself and didn't tell me much about it."

"Did he ever mention the name Leslie Baker to you?"

"If he did, I don't recall it."

"Did he bring up anyone's name from the building he moved into?" Claire asked.

"Hmm. It was such a long time ago." Lucy-Lin's brow furrowed as she tried to remember.

"Henry Prior?" Claire asked. "Amy Wonder?"

Lucy-Lin made eye contact with Claire. "Amy Wonder. That's a name I think I would remember, if I'd heard it."

"How about Peter Safer?"

"That sounds familiar." The doctor tilted her head in question. "But, I don't know if I heard it from Allen or not. Probably not." After tilting her bottle of juice to her mouth and finishing it off, she set it down and checked the wall clock. "I need to go in a minute." She crumpled her napkin into a ball and placed it on the lunch tray.

"Did Allen ever mention if someone in the building was selling to him?" Claire wished that something helpful might come from the discussion.

Lucy-Lin started to shake her head, but then her eyes seemed to sharpen. "You know ... one night, I went to Allen's place after I'd been at a meeting in Cambridge. He wasn't expecting me. His door was open a little and I pushed it and looked into the living room as I knocked on the doorframe. Allen was very surprised to see me and he stood up from the sofa and quickly picked things up from the table." She made a sour face. "There was another guy in the room with him. I knew Allen was buying drugs from him. The guy scurried away, then Allen and I had a huge fight."

"Do you remember what the guy looked like?" Claire leaned forward a little, eager to hear if the woman would be able to recall any details about the man.

"I was so angry at Allen I barely looked at the guy in the room." Lucy-Lin shook her head as the scene re-played in her head. Glancing up at the clock again, she stood and gathered her things. "I'm sorry. I have to scoot. I'm late already."

Claire thanked the woman for her time and stood up to go.

They shook hands and Lucy-Lin picked up her tray and started away. Before taking four steps, she stopped and turned back. "Claire. That guy. The drug dealer. I'm pretty sure he had an English accent."

Claire's heart skipped a beat. *Peter Safer?*

CLAIRE MET Nicole at the Boston Common and while the Corgis raced over the grass playing with the other dogs, the young women settled on a bench in the sun.

After Claire relayed the information she'd gathered from Dr. Lucy-Lin Zhou, Nicole's head snapped around when her friend brought up the part about the drug dealer having an English accent.

"An English accent?" Nicole stared at Claire. "The dealer must have been Peter Safer. Wow. I can't believe it. Peter Safer was selling drugs. Didn't Jill Lansing mention seeing Peter standing at Allen Day's room chatting with him sometimes?"

"She did say that, yes."

Nicole was wide-eyed. "They must have been talking about drugs. Peter must have been selling all over the city."

"At the very least, it seems he was selling to the grad students," Claire said.

"I wonder if Leslie knew about Peter's part-time job." Nicole watched as the group of dogs tore past them and ran around the common.

Claire's heart pounded. "Could Peter being a dealer have contributed to Leslie's murder? Did someone kill her because she was Peter's girlfriend? Did someone kill her to get back at Peter for something?"

Nicole's eyes were sad. "Was any of this in Marty's file notes?"

"I didn't see it."

"Neither did I. We need to tell Marty about this development." Nicole looked at her friend. "How will we figure this out? If someone involved in the drug trade from thirty-three years ago killed Leslie, how will we find out who it was?"

Claire let out a sigh. "We could talk to Peter Safer again."

Nicole frowned and said, "Why do I think he won't agree to that?"

"Because, he probably won't," Claire said.

Nicole's eyes narrowed. "We could ambush him."

Claire looked at her friend for clarification.

"We could hang around outside Safer's office building and approach him when he comes out. We've done it before with other people."

"Remember how those times worked out?" Claire asked with a frown. "The usual reaction is for the person to get angry with us and storm away."

"Any other suggestions?"

"What if we do a modified version of an ambush. We could go to his office and ask to meet with him."

Nicole raised an eyebrow. "Right. He'll say no ... or his secretary will say no and then we'll get shooed out of the place."

"We could bring Ian."

"Would he come with us?" Nicole asked hopefully.

"I'll talk to him about it." Claire rubbed her eyes. "I'm exhausted. This case is like running in circles."

Nicole asked, "Do you think the police knew Peter Safer was selling drugs back then?"

"Do they usually know who the people are who deal drugs?"

"It seems like they do," Nicole said. "Or is that just something that goes on now? Did the cops know things like that years ago?"

"I have no idea," Claire said.

Nicole said, "If the police knew Safer was selling drugs and his girlfriend got murdered, wouldn't they suspect a link to the drug world? Like it was someone getting revenge on Peter for something?"

"It certainly puts a different twist on things." Claire kneaded at the tight muscles in her neck. "It seems like the police would investigate that link. Maybe they did and there was nothing there. It could be there was no link at all between the murder and drugs."

Nicole eyed her friend. "There might be someone who could answer some of these questions."

"Who?" Claire asked.

"Our favorite criminal who works out of a South End bar."

Claire rolled her eyes and groaned.

"It might be worth paying Mr. Cooney a visit,

however painful it may be," Nicole said. "He seems to know just about everything that goes on around these parts."

"You know he doesn't give anything away for free," Claire warned. "And he is very expensive."

"Well, I know someone who has plenty of money and this is a good cause." Nicole winked.

Claire shook her head and let out another groan. "I'll stop at the bank on my way home."

21

Claire carried a tray of lemon cookies to the front of the shop and slipped it into the glass display case before making a mocha latte for a customer. When she finished, she placed it on the counter, clicked on the lid, and handed it to the man with a smile. Someone came in through the chocolate shop's front door as the customer exited, and when Claire saw who it was, her eyes went wide.

Amy Wonder stood just inside the door with her eyes flicking around the space and when she noticed Claire behind the counter, she nodded to her and gave a little smile as she approached the pastry counter. Despite the woman's smile, Claire could see by Amy's movements and facial expression that she was worried or nervous.

"What a pleasant surprise." Claire walked around the pastry cases and gestured to an open table. "Would you like to sit?"

"I hope I'm not disturbing you." A tenseness showed in Amy's eyes. "Do you have a few minutes to talk?"

When they sat down at a corner table, Amy explained, "Ever since we met, things have been swirling through my mind about the cold case. Bits of conversations, images of things I did, feelings from the past, they pop into my head at random moments. Talking with you about Leslie's murder stirred up old memories and brought a bunch of things back to the surface."

Claire listened intently knowing Amy must have something to tell her. She gave the woman a nod. "That can happen. It's common in situations like this."

"I wanted to talk to you more about Leslie," Amy said.

"You remembered some things?" Claire asked.

"You recall we talked about Professor Ambrose's trowel?" Amy asked. "You know how you get little signals or messages from your body when you sense something isn't right? Well, some feelings surfaced, nothing major or earth-shattering, but it started to pick at me a little and I decided I'd talk to you and you can decide if it's anything."

Claire didn't want to interrupt in any way, so she just nodded again and said, "Sure."

"You brought up the trowel. When we were packing to leave Iraq, I remembered Leslie telling me that Professor Ambrose had given her the trowel. At the time, something about it seemed off. It was the way Leslie said the words, her tone of voice. I brushed it off back then, but it's been playing over and over in my head."

Amy took a quick sip from the beverage Claire had brought over when they went to the table. Claire thought she noticed the woman's fingers trembling.

Amy went on, "Ambrose was enthralled with Leslie, always flirting with her, always hanging around her. I was glad he wasn't acting that way with me ... he seemed like a real pain. His behavior seemed so exhausting that I felt bad for Leslie. Ambrose was always showing up wherever Leslie was, monopolizing her, right up in her face. He was like a pesky puppy." Amy let out a soft groan.

"Leslie enjoyed him though, didn't she?" Claire asked.

"Leslie did enjoy him initially, but as the weeks went on, I noticed she became less interested in his constant attention."

"Did she ever say anything to you about Ambrose?"

"Occasionally, she'd mutter something like 'here he comes again' or when she was tired, she wouldn't smile at his comments or laugh at his jokes ... which seemed to irk Ambrose."

"Do you think Ambrose gave her the trowel to gain her affection?" Claire asked.

Amy sat quietly for a few moments. "I don't know if Ambrose gave her the trowel or not. If I had to make a guess, I'd say he *didn't* give it to her."

"You think Leslie took it from him?" Claire kept the surprise from showing in her voice.

"I think it's possible."

Claire asked, "Why do you think she took it?"

"There was some tension between them during the last days of the dig," Amy said.

"Not getting along?" Claire suspected it was more than that.

"A few days before we left Iraq, I heard an argument. Leslie was letting Ambrose have it. She kept her voice low, I assume so as not to call attention to their interaction, but she was angry. Really angry. It sounded like she was hissing venom at him."

"Did you hear what she was saying to him?" Claire hoped that Amy had been close enough to hear Leslie's words.

"Some, not much." Amy gripped her cup. "I'm pretty sure Ambrose made a move on Leslie and kissed her. Leslie was ranting at him about invading her personal space and that she did not consent to be kissed and she should file a complaint against him for harassment."

Amy let out a breath. "I got a quick look at them as I passed by the window. Leslie's body language said it all. She wasn't afraid of Ambrose, she was practically in his face. Ambrose looked horrified, but something else was mixed in ... it looked a lot like suppressed rage. I paused for a second in case Leslie needed help, but it was clear she was in charge of the situation. I scurried away."

"Did you talk to her about the argument?" Claire asked.

"I brought it up the next night. Leslie dismissed it. She said something about how you have to be careful being friendly with men because they let it go to their heads and misinterpret it as attraction and think they're entitled to you. Leslie said she had to be more careful in the future. She had to be on her guard." Amy shook her head sadly and her eyes misted over. "I guess she let her guard down the night she was killed."

Amy collected herself and brushed her hand over her face. "I'm not accusing anyone of anything. I wanted to tell you what I remembered. Lots of men were attracted to Leslie like Ambrose was." Amy looked Claire in the eye. "Maybe one of them didn't care to be refused and let his anger get the best of him."

"How were things between Leslie and Ambrose after the incident?"

"Ambrose acted his usual playful self, but it almost seemed forced. It had an edge to it. No one else would pick up on it. I only did because I witnessed part of the argument."

"How did Leslie act?"

"She tried to be herself, but I noticed a coolness towards Ambrose. Again, they both tried to act like everything was the same as always. I don't think anyone else noticed a thing."

"Do you think Ambrose pursued Leslie once they were back in the States?" Claire asked.

Amy said, "Leslie told me she met with Ambrose

once at a coffee shop to chat. When I asked how it went, all she said was that he was the same as always."

"Did she see him again after that?"

"I have no idea. I don't see what the point would be. Ambrose was married. He made a move on Leslie and she rebuffed him. It was clear what he wanted. Why bother to see him? Wouldn't that only encourage him?"

"Unless he apologized and wanted to be friends," Claire suggested.

"That wasn't the impression I got from Ambrose."

"Did you see Professor Ambrose after Iraq?"

"I saw him at a get-together a month or so after we returned from Iraq. I arrived late to the restaurant so I didn't have a chance to talk to him. I also saw him briefly at Leslie's memorial service. I had no interest in speaking with him. I was distraught over Leslie and didn't feel like making small talk so I avoided him."

Claire and Amy sat in silence for a few moments.

Claire asked softly, "Do you mind if I ask why you and Henry Prior broke up?"

Amy's eyebrow raised for a second. "We were both devastated by what happened to Leslie. We didn't have much strength to give to each other ... we were impatient and needy and unable to help anyone but ourselves. It was a struggle to drag myself through my days. I never thought I'd feel normal again. I moved to another building. Jill moved in with her boyfriend."

"Did Henry move, too?"

"Henry stayed in his apartment. Maybe all the new people who moved in were enough of a change for him so he stayed put." Amy shrugged.

"Did you initiate the breakup with Henry?"

"I did. Henry didn't seem to care."

"Really? You'd been together for a while, hadn't you?"

"A couple of years." Amy sighed and looked out the window to the busy sidewalk outside the shop. "I thought Henry was so together, so smart. He knew about so many different fields, he was able to debate anyone on any subject. I began to see that his interest in debate wasn't an indication of his intelligence needing an outlet. In Henry's case, it was a need to dominate other people and to always, always be right." The woman looked back at Claire. "I decided those weren't very attractive characteristics."

Claire took a deep breath and asked, "Did Henry take drugs?"

Amy blinked several times and stared at Claire. "No, never."

"Did you know anyone who was selling drugs to people in your building?"

"Selling? No. Are you trying to figure out where Allen Day got his drugs?" Amy's eyes went wide. "You don't think Henry was selling, do you?"

"No, I don't think it was Henry." Claire asked, "Was Henry friendly with Peter Safer, Jill, and Leslie?"

"Yes, he was. Henry could be a lot fun ... when he wasn't in one of his belligerent moods," Amy said.

"Was Henry the type who would hold a grudge over something?"

"I suppose sometimes, he did."

"Did Leslie ever rub Henry the wrong way?"

Amy's face hardened. "On the contrary. Henry had a thing for Leslie. He always tried a little too hard when she was around. I caught him more than once trying to flirt with her. That was another reason I broke up with him. I did not want to live my life with a man with a roving eye."

"Did Leslie encourage Henry's flirtation?" Claire asked.

"I'm sure Henry would have been happy to have

had a little fling with Leslie, but she certainly had no interest in him."

"Could Henry have been so angry that Leslie wouldn't play his game that he...."

"Killed her?" Amy finished Claire's sentence and then gave a sad shrug. "Only Henry ... and Leslie ... know the answer to that question."

22

When Claire entered the hospital atrium and stepped out of the elevator, a man walked by and was about to pass Claire when he stopped and turned.

"Claire?" Dr. Henry Prior adjusted his tortoiseshell eyeglasses.

Claire smiled and walked over to Prior. "I was actually here looking for you. I left work a little while ago and decided on a whim to take a chance and see if you had a few minutes so I took a cab over."

"How can I help?" Prior asked.

"I had a few things to talk to you about." Claire looked around for somewhere they could sit.

"Come to my office." Prior gestured down the hall. "I can only spare a bit of time."

"I don't think it will take long."

Claire followed Prior into his office and took the same seat as the last time she visited the doctor. "I wanted to chat briefly about the young man who lived in the apartment across from you, Allen Day."

One of Prior's eyebrows raised. "Allen Day? I hardly knew him. I barely spoke to the poor man."

"He died from an overdose," Claire said.

"Yes. A tragedy."

"Do you know where Mr. Day got his drugs? Did you ever see anyone stop by Day's apartment and stay only briefly?" Claire watched Prior's face closely for a reaction wondering if he knew Peter Safer might have been selling drugs.

"I didn't notice anything. I barely saw the man. He was never around. I have no idea who was selling Day the drugs." Prior picked up a pencil from his desk and rolled it between his fingers. "What does that have to do with Leslie?"

"We're trying to establish motive," Claire said. "A young man died from an overdose a few doors down from Leslie's apartment. It could very well have implications."

Prior sat straight. "Surely, you don't think Leslie was a drug dealer?"

Claire shook her head. "I don't have any reason to think that, but if drugs were bought and sold in the building, Leslie may have witnessed something she shouldn't have and it may have caused repercussions. You never saw anything going on in the building related to drugs?"

"I did not."

"Did your friends on your floor do drugs?"

"They did not."

"I have to ask and I apologize, but did you take drugs?" Claire asked.

"Never. That wasn't my thing. In those days, I preferred a few beers when I wanted to relax."

"Did you consider yourself friends with Peter Safer?"

Prior's shoulder twitched. "Friendly, I suppose is the way I'd describe it. We didn't socialize outside of the building. We didn't go to events together or anything like that. We had different social circles. We hung out in Amy's apartment and when Peter and Leslie were around, they'd join us."

Claire gave a nod. "And what about Leslie? Did you consider her a friend?"

"I'd say the same thing about Leslie as I did about Peter. We were friendly."

"Why do you think Amy broke off her relationship with you?" Claire asked.

Prior's cheeks seemed to tinge pink. "I was the one who initiated the breakup. We'd grown apart. We couldn't connect anymore."

"Were you in a monogamous relationship with Amy?"

Prior smirked. "It was a long time ago. I was young and foolish."

Claire kept her voice even being sure not to use an accusatory tone. "Did you ever try to start something with Leslie?"

"Leslie was a beautiful girl. I wouldn't have said no if she was interested."

"Was she interested?"

"I never asked her." Prior had a wide grin on his face that made Claire dislike him.

"When you left Amy's apartment to go home that night, was anyone hanging around in the hallway? Did you see anyone in the hall you were unfamiliar with?"

"I don't recall seeing anyone."

Claire removed an old photograph of Malden

Ambrose from her bag. “Do you recognize this man?”

Prior moved his glasses up his nose and leaned closer to the photo. “I don't know him. Who is he?”

“He was a professor on the dig that Leslie was on in Iraq. They became friends.”

Prior's eyes brightened. “Friends? Or ... friendly?”

“I don't believe they had a relationship. It was strictly a friendly acquaintance,” Claire said. “Do you remember ever seeing the man with Leslie? Seeing him around the building?”

“He looks like a thousand other guys. Nothing stands out. Who knows? I may have passed him on the street. I wouldn't remember.”

“You never met him then?”

“Not that I recall.”

“Had you been in Leslie's apartment?”

“Sure. We socialized in all the apartments. Mostly, we would gather in Jill and Amy's place because it was bigger.”

“Who do you think killed Leslie?” Claire asked.

Prior lifted his hands, palms to the ceiling. “I have no idea.”

When Claire reached down to put the photo of

Malden Ambrose back in her bag, she noticed something hanging on the wall that sent a shiver over her skin. A framed, small red, orange, and blue kilim rug about three feet by four feet hung on the wall. Her eyes bored into it for almost a half minute.

"That wasn't here the last time I visited you," Claire said with her eyes still glued to the rug.

"It was sent out to be cleaned." Prior shifted nervously in his seat.

Claire stood up and leaned forward to get a good look at the piece. "It's a beautiful textile. The colors are wonderful."

"Thank you," Prior said.

Claire waited for Prior to give some information about the rug, but he said nothing. She faced the man. "Where did you get it?"

"From a friend."

"It's a striking piece," Claire said. "What is the country of origin?"

"I believe it came from the Middle East, I'm not sure which country."

"Have you had it for a long time?"

"A few years," Prior told her.

Claire had a strong feeling that Prior was lying. "Didn't Leslie have a textile like this?"

"She did, yes."

Claire waited, but Prior said nothing more. "Was this Leslie's piece?"

Prior looked like he was about to dismiss the notion, but he stuck out his chin and said, "It was."

Claire returned to her seat with a pleasant smile. "How did you get hold of it?"

"I asked a police officer if I might have it."

You asked for the rug on the day of the murder?" Claire asked.

"Yes," Prior said.

"Wasn't the textile one of the things that had been placed on top of Leslie's body?"

"I believe it was."

"And the police officer had no problem with you removing it from the crime scene?"

"He said I could have it." Prior's voice held a tone of defiance.

"Why did you want it?" Claire held the man's eyes.

"I thought it was a lovely piece," Prior said in his defense. "I'd admired it for a while. Leslie was dead, she didn't have any use for it and I thought it would be nice to remember her by."

"You didn't think it best to leave it at the crime scene until everything was processed?" Claire asked.

"I didn't think of it, really. The officer said it was okay to take it so I did."

"What about her parents? Might they have wanted it?"

"I don't know. No one seemed to care." Prior had a look on his face that said he had no idea why Claire was making a big deal over taking the textile. "I had it framed. I hung it on my apartment wall until I moved it here."

"Someone took an excavation hammer from Leslie's bedroom," Claire stated.

"That was me," Prior admitted.

Claire couldn't help the look of surprise that rushed over her face. "You took the hammer?"

Prior nodded.

"Why?"

"I didn't think anyone would want it."

"It might have been the murder weapon," Claire said leaning forward in her chair. She couldn't believe someone would be so naïve to take an object that might have killed the woman. "Did it have blood on it?"

"No, of course not."

"Where was it in the room?"

"On the bookcase near the bed."

"There wasn't any blood spatter that hit the

bookcase?"

"No, there wasn't. I did nothing wrong." Prior's voice was getting louder. "I took the two objects with permission."

"I don't understand why police would release two objects from a murder scene," Claire said. "Especially before *processing* the scene."

"I can't answer for the police."

"Where is the hammer now?"

"The police retrieved it from me. I voluntarily gave it up." Prior crossed his arms over his chest. "I don't know what the fuss is over this."

"The fuss?" Claire asked. "The fuss is that you walked into a crime scene and removed two items that may have contained evidence. You're a smart man, Dr. Prior. What possessed you to do that? Didn't you think about the evidence?"

"Honestly, no. The police knew what they were doing. I didn't take the things without asking."

"I'm surprised the police didn't consider you a suspect for removing evidence from the room."

"Perhaps they did." Prior leaned an elbow on his desk with a satisfied smile. "But they couldn't find any evidence *against me*."

Maybe because you took the available evidence from the room. Claire stood, looked at Leslie's rug hanging on the wall, and glanced back at Prior with disgust. "Thank you for talking with me."

"Come back anytime," Prior said. "Always happy to help."

Claire wanted to slap the man, but instead, she spoke through gritted teeth as she left the office, "I appreciate it."

23

Doing research from his apartment, Marty was able to track down Malden Ambrose's ex-wife, Sheila Mathers, and although the woman was initially reluctant to be interviewed, she finally relented under Marty's genial prodding. He set up a time and date and forwarded the information to Claire.

After they closed the chocolate shop for the day, Nicole and Claire hurried up the stairs of the Boston Public Library and made their way to the library's café where they found Ms. Mathers at a table working at her laptop. When she noticed the two young women, she waved them over to the table.

"I'm Sheila. Please sit."

After introductions and a bit of chit-chat, they

turned attention to the cold case of Leslie Baker's murder.

Sheila, in her early sixties, was well-dressed in a skirt and blazer, and had short blond hair cut stylishly around her face framing high cheek bones and beautiful skin. "Your associate, Marty Wyatt, has a winning personality. He can also make quite a compelling argument about why I needed to meet with you."

Claire chuckled. "Marty can be very persuasive."

"You want to talk to me about Malden in connection to that young woman's death," Sheila stated.

Nicole explained, "We'd like to ask some questions about your former husband and some of his professional contacts. He had been to Iraq on a dig with Leslie Baker."

"Yes, he went on the expedition as part of a three-university effort." Sheila spoke matter-of-factly.

"Did he talk about Leslie to you?"

"He talked about many of the people on the dig. Malden enjoyed the group. He told me it was one of the best trips he'd been on."

"Did he seem especially fond of any of the people?" Claire asked.

Sheila leveled her eyes at the young women. "Do you mean romantically?"

"Was he romantically involved with someone on the dig?" Nicole asked with surprise.

"Whenever Malden went on trips, he was either involved with someone who was there or he wanted to be involved with someone who was there." Sheila's lips pinched together. "Malden was a ladies man. In other words, a cheater, and not just any kind of cheater, but an Olympic gold medal winning cheater. World-class. A champ."

"And you knew about his behavior back then?"

"I suspected," Sheila said. "I was young, naïve. We were newly married when he went to Iraq. I thought Malden needed some time to settle down, settle into married life. I was sure he loved me, but he had this terrible need to follow his emotions. He couldn't stop himself. We divorced about two years after we married. It was foolish of me to think he would change."

"Malden was involved with someone in Iraq?" Claire asked again.

"My impression was that Malden tried to get cozy with Leslie Baker, but she wasn't having any of it. Malden never took well to being rejected. It seemed to fuel his desire to get what he wanted. The man was sick. I wouldn't put up with it."

"Did he tell you about his interest in Leslie?" Nicole was appalled to think Malden would discuss his escapades with his wife.

"Not outright, but I was good at reading between the lines. I caught him calling her number when they returned to the States. I followed him once to Harvard Square and saw him meet Leslie at a coffee shop. I know it sounds awful to snoop on someone, but when you have suspicions, well, I had to see for myself."

"It doesn't sound awful at all," Claire reassured the woman that they understood.

"Malden usually cheated with someone and then moved on rather quickly to the next pursuit. Leslie rebuffing him seemed to drive him crazy. I don't know if it was because he was desperate to have her or if the act of rejection itself was the cause for his obsession."

"He was obsessed with Leslie?" Nicole asked.

Sheila let out a soft sigh. "He sure was. I found a folder in his office. I was snooping, yes. It was full of pictures of Leslie. Notes about her: about her birthdate, where she was from, her friends, some quotes Malden attributed to her." The woman shook her head slowly. "I have to admit when I found those notes, I nearly passed out. It was so odd to find your husband's collection of things about another woman. It was frightening."

"Was Malden ever violent?"

"No. I never saw any physical violence, although Malden could be verbally rude, superior, dismissive."

"Did you confront him about the notes you found?" Claire asked.

"I did not. If it happened now, I certainly would, but back then, I was unsure of myself. I had thoughts that if I was a better wife, then he wouldn't be straying. Ridiculous, of course, but that's what went through my mind." Sheila scoffed. "Now? I'd string that no-good cheater up. I'd kick his behind right out the door, no second chances. Adios and good riddance."

"Do you keep in touch with Malden?" Nicole questioned.

Sheila laughed. "I haven't seen him in decades. Why would I bother? We didn't have children together. We dissolved our marriage. The only person Malden cares about is himself. I want nothing to do with him." The woman's face softened. "I remarried a few years later to a lovely man I met through a friend. He is the kindest, most caring soul on the planet. My best friend, even after all these years. We have three wonderful children. I'm very lucky."

Claire smiled at Sheila, sincerely happy that she'd found such a good man and had made a rich and rewarding life with him.

"Malden tried to see Leslie many times." Sheila leaned her arms on the table. "I hired a private detective."

"You did?" Nicole's eyes widened and a big smile crossed her face.

"I wanted to gather information on Malden in order to have proof of reason for divorce. I hired a man to follow him. It sounds very cloak and dagger, but it proved to me that I wasn't blowing things out of proportion. Right after coming back from Iraq, Malden spent a couple of days a week trying to meet with Leslie. Sometimes, he'd go where he thought she would be to try to run into her. He even went to her apartment twice to see if he could talk to her."

"Did he find her? Would she talk to him?"

"The private investigator told me Malden was never successful in bumping into Leslie so he started calling her. Leslie had no idea that Malden was on such a hunt for her. They met up a few times at coffee shops. Leslie always left him and went home or to a class. She never invited Malden to her place. The PI told me he pitied Malden." Sheila made a face. "My feelings about Malden ran more towards fury and disgust."

"We were told that Malden had an archaeological tool, a trowel with mother-of-pearl inset in the handle," Claire said.

"He did, yes. Early in our marriage, I gave him that set as a present."

"The trowel ended up in Leslie Baker's possession," Nicole told Sheila. "We were told she left Iraq with it."

Sheila's forehead furrowed and she tilted her head slightly to the side. "Oh, really? I asked Malden about that trowel. He told me he lost it in Iraq. He gave it to Leslie?"

"We aren't sure if he gave it to her or if she took it from him." Claire told Sheila they'd heard that Malden made an unwelcome advance towards Leslie while in Iraq and that Leslie had told him in no uncertain terms to back off. "We wonder if Leslie took the trowel from Malden out of anger."

"That's an interesting theory." Sheila nodded. "Maybe it was a nonverbal message from Leslie to Malden not to mess with her."

"That could be," Nicole said. "Malden must have taken the news about Leslie's murder hard."

"He certainly did. He didn't get out of bed for two days, but dear Malden had a rather miraculous recovery. He was back on the prowl about two weeks later chasing after an undergraduate young woman in one of his summer classes. Malden had better luck with younger woman ... freshmen, sophomores. I think they were flattered by the professor's attention." Sheila gave a disgusted shake of her head. "Malden was a handsome man. He could be very charming. The undergrads were much easier for him."

"Where was Malden the night Leslie was killed?" Nicole asked.

Sheila looked at Nicole and, flustered, blinked several times before saying, "Where was he? Do you think Malden had something to do with Leslie's death?" She raised her hand to her mouth. "Oh. I never considered such a thing. Malden? I don't think so. Malden was never violent."

"Did the police interview Malden?" Claire asked.

"No, they didn't," Sheila said. "Why would they? The private investigator informed me that Malden had given up on Leslie about two months before she was murdered."

"Was Malden at home that night?" Nicole asked the question again.

"Yes. I had a migraine that day. It was a bad one. Malden was very nice to me. He brought me cold cloths for my forehead, glasses of water, made sure the shades were pulled to keep out the sunlight. I'd get a migraine every few months. I'd sleep for about twenty-four hours after it hit me."

"How did you find out Leslie had been killed?" Claire asked.

"Malden told me. He came into my room in the afternoon. I'd been asleep for hours. He was crying. He told me that the television news was reporting a murder in the building Leslie lived in. The dead girl's description fit Leslie." Sheila looked down at her hands. "I actually felt bad for Malden." She lifted her eyes. "For a couple of hours anyway."

As she listened to Sheila tell about the day Leslie was killed, Claire felt little buzzes of electricity nipping at her skin. *Was Malden really at home that night?*

24

For two hours of the late afternoon, Claire and Nicole sat outside at a café's patio across from Peter Safer's office building waiting for the man to emerge. When he did not appear, they worried he'd exited a different way so Nicole made a call to the financial firm asking for Mr. Safer to find out if he was still there or not. The secretary-receptionist explained that Safer had left for the day and suggested Nicole leave a message, but she declined to do so.

"He's gone for the day." Nicole rolled her eyes as she clicked off from the call. "We've been sitting here for nothing." Standing up, Nicole asked Claire if she wanted to grab a drink at the upscale bar where they'd met Safer for a chat a couple of days ago.

On entering the establishment, it took a few seconds for their eyes to adjust to the subdued lighting and when she could see clearly, Claire elbowed Nicole and nodded across the room. "Look who's here."

"Well, well." Nicole spotted Peter Safer sitting on a stool at the end of the bar with his back against the granite counter and a glass in one of his hands. She winked at Claire. "Why don't we go say hello."

When Safer saw the two young women approaching, he stiffened and his head moved from side to side as if he was looking for an exit.

"Hello, Mr. Safer," Nicole said with a wide smile. "Nice to see you again."

Claire came up on Nicole's left and gave the man a nod. "Can we join you?"

"No." Safer slurred the word despite it having only a consonant and a vowel and being only one, lonely syllable.

"Were we really such unpleasant company?" Nicole slid onto the stool next to the man and faced him.

"Yes, you were." Somehow, Safer's short sentence came out more clearly than his previous one-word utterance.

Claire stepped over to stand closer to Safer as if

she, the man, and Nicole were old friends who'd decided to visit the bar together after a school reunion. "We called your office and they told us you'd finished for the day."

"So you decided to come by and harass me again?" Safer's words ran together in a long mush of sounds.

"We only had a conversation last time we met." Claire signaled the bartender. "I'm sorry to hear you thought we were bothering you. That wasn't what we intended."

Safer lifted his rheumy eyes and narrowed his gaze to better focus on Claire. "What did you intend?"

"To gather information to help bring Leslie's killer to justice." Nicole accepted a drink from the bartender and passed one to Claire.

"Your hope is the same as ours, I believe," Claire said. "To solve Leslie's murder."

"You'll never be able to do that." Safer watched the dark liquid making waves in his glass from his shaky hand.

"Why not?" Claire held her wine glass without drinking from it.

"It's been too long," Safer muttered. "Evidence is gone. People have given up."

"We haven't given up," Claire told him. "We want justice for Leslie."

"Leslie." Safer said the word as a mix of a moan and a sigh.

Claire and Nicole exchanged a quick look and waited for the man to say more. When he only sat glumly on the stool, Claire asked, "Did you say something?"

"Leslie. I should have been more careful." Safer shifted his eyes to the young women. "Did I do something?"

A cold shiver ran through Claire. "What do you mean?"

His eyes heavy with sadness, Safer whispered, "I'm afraid ... I'm afraid I might have caused her death."

Claire realized that Safer was drunker than she thought, but she knew she had to carefully choose her words or risk spooking the man. "How would that have happened?"

"I was a fool back then." Safer took a huge gulp from his glass and then scoffed. "I thought I knew what I was doing."

"But...?" Nicole prompted.

"But, I was naïve and simple." Safer swiveled his stool a little so he could set his glass on the countertop. "I've been thinking about this over and over. Ever since I talked to you, my head has been spinning. I can't stop thinking. I was going to call you."

"About Leslie?" Claire asked.

"I broke the law back then," Safer told them.

"Did you?" Claire eyed the man.

"You know what I did? Have you uncovered that bit of information yet?" Safer looked from Claire to Nicole and back again, and when he leaned towards them, he wobbled so mightily that Claire's arm shot out in case he began to tumble from his perch. Safer regained his equilibrium and in a low voice, he said, "I sold drugs."

Claire's eyes went wide. She couldn't believe Safer had just revealed that he was once a drug dealer. "You sold drugs?" Her tone of voice held such interest that Safer went on.

"Not for long," the man said. "Maybe just over a year. A year and a half at the most. I don't really remember exactly how long I did it."

"Why did you sell?" Nicole asked.

"For the money," Safer said with an impatient tone. "I grew up poor. We didn't have any money. Selling was quick, easy, fast cash. I was rolling in it. I loved it."

"What made you stop?" Claire eyed the man.

Safer's face drooped and he got a faraway look in his eyes. "I sold to a guy who lived on Leslie's floor. Allen Day, a medical student. He overdosed." Safer almost winced. "He died ... because I sold him the drugs." Rubbing his forehead, the man looked down at his hands and then lifted his gaze to the young women. "Leslie was so upset. She was furious with me. She ranted at me to stop selling. I was distraught. Not because Leslie was having a fit ... no, I was distraught because due to my actions, a young man was dead."

"Did you tell the police you were selling drugs when they interviewed you after Leslie's death?" Claire asked.

Safer hung his head. "No. I was afraid. I was afraid they'd charge me for Allen Day's death, so I kept quiet. I assumed they might know I was selling from their contacts, but they never mentioned it, so neither did I."

Claire asked softly, "Did you supply Leslie with drugs?"

Safer's head popped up. "Leslie? Never. She didn't do drugs."

"Why do you think you caused Leslie's death?" Nicole asked.

Safer's shoulders dipped a little. "I worked for a

guy, a guy who ran a tight ship. I got introduced to him through an acquaintance and he took a chance on me. I think he liked that I had easy access to lots of students, some of whom had very deep pockets."

"This guy was your supplier?" Claire asked.

Safer gave a quick nod. "And woe to anyone who crossed him." Letting out a long, slow breath, he went on. "When I told the guy I wanted out, he beat me up. Well, *he* didn't. His goons did. The guy told me I wasn't going anywhere. I said I'd do one more month and then I was out."

"He agreed?" Nicole asked.

"Not really. I figured I wouldn't try to move much product and this guy would eventually cut me loose."

"What does this have to do with Leslie?" Claire asked.

"I'm afraid this guy killed Leslie to get back at me." Safer's hands started to shake. "I'm afraid he killed her to send me a message."

"Why do you think so?" Claire wasn't convinced.

"I was at home after seeing Leslie the night she got killed. I got a call from someone in her building who wanted to buy. I had some product left and wanted to unload it so I agreed to go back to the building and meet the person." Safer reached for his glass and downed the remaining liquid. "I sold the stuff to someone on the fourth floor of Leslie's building. It was the last of my stash. I decided that was it, no more involvement with drugs. As I was heading out, my 'boss' met me in the stairwell. We had words. He said if I quit on him, he'd have someone pay me a visit. I told him I didn't care, I was done, send whoever he wanted. The guy got up in my face and whispered that I'd be sorry. I can still feel his breath on my skin."

"You think this guy killed Leslie?" Nicole asked.

"He was in Leslie's building that night. I left him in there. I stormed out and went home. When I returned to Leslie's the next day, she was dead."

"That doesn't mean her death was caused by this drug guy," Claire spoke gently.

"It was him," Safer almost hissed. "He did it to get back at me. He knew I was seeing Leslie."

"Didn't you tell us that your relationship with Leslie was off when she got killed?" Claire asked. "Hadn't she put you in the *friend* category at that time?"

"She had, yes, but this guy knew I dated Leslie."

"Why didn't you tell the police your suspicions?" Nicole asked.

Safer's face hardened. "Because I figured I'd be

next, that's why. I thought if I told the cops about the guy, then he'd kill me, too."

Claire asked, "Why would this guy have spread red ochre around Leslie's body and in her room?"

"I don't know. Maybe he knew what Leslie was studying. Maybe he knew ancient burial rites. How do I know why he did it?"

"Did you see this man again?" Claire asked.

"No."

"Not around the university? Somewhere in Cambridge?" Nicole questioned.

"I didn't see him again." Safer leveled his eyes at Nicole. "If this guy didn't want to be seen, then he wasn't seen."

"What was this man's name?" Claire asked.

"It doesn't matter," Safer muttered.

"Why doesn't it matter?" Nicole asked. "If he's around, then the police can pick him up and question him."

"They can't. The guy died." Safer's jaw muscles tightened. "He got killed in a bar brawl."

"You think this guy is responsible for Leslie's murder?" Claire locked eyes with Safer.

"Yes, I do."

"Will you go talk to the police? Tell them what you think?"

"I will not."

"Why not?" Claire asked.

"I won't admit to selling drugs." Safer sat up to his full height. "I won't be portrayed in a news story as the drug-selling idiot. I have clients. I have a business. I have a reputation. Absolutely not. I won't be dragged through the mud after all I've worked for and built. I will *not* go to the police."

"Why did you tell us this then?" Nicole asked.

"So you'll stop barking up the wrong tree." Safer stared at Nicole. "The killer is dead. Stop wasting your time."

Claire eyed the man. *Are you sure we're wasting our time?*

25

Claire, Robby, and Nicole worked in the kitchen of the chocolate shop mixing and baking some items for the next day.

"I locked the front door and turned the 'Closed' sign around so nobody will come in while we're working," Robby said as he creamed butter and sugar in a big bowl.

"Good," Nicole said. "I don't want anyone eavesdropping on our conversation."

Claire gave Robby a summary of her and Nicole's meeting with Peter Safer at the bar last evening.

"Sounds like Mr. Safer is trying to divert attention away from himself," Robby announced.

"I wondered the very same thing." Claire added bits of shaved chocolate to the mixture she was working on. "At times, Safer seemed sincere in his emotion and other times, I thought he was doing a great job of throwing suspicion off of himself and onto someone else."

"Clever," Robby scowled. "Where does Dr. Weirdo stand in the list of suspects?" Claire's young co-worker had given the nickname to Dr. Henry Prior after hearing the man took things from the murder scene shortly after Leslie had died.

Claire tried to suppress a smile. "He's at the top of the list along with Peter Safer and Professor Ambrose."

"A trio of strange men." Robby poured the mixture into two loaf pans. "Didn't Leslie Baker hang around with any normal guys?"

"She probably did, but these three have my attention," Claire said.

Robby eyed the woman working next to him. "Does Clairvoyant Claire have a *feeling* about which one of the trio is guilty?"

Claire ignored the remark about being clairvoyant. "Not exactly."

"No ideas?" Robby asked.

"Ever since this thing started, I've had a nagging sense that Leslie knew her killer." Claire scooped small mounds of batter onto cookie sheets.

Nicole had been working quietly while listening to Claire and Robby discuss the case. "I wonder if Professor Ambrose has any insight into Peter Safer or Henry Prior's relationship with Leslie. It sounded like Leslie and Ambrose got along great at the start of the dig, until Ambrose developed feelings for her. I bet Leslie felt like it was safe to have a friendship with Ambrose because he was married. She might have confided in Ambrose about Safer or Prior or someone else."

"Ambrose claimed to know nothing when we talked to him," Claire pointed out.

"That could be untrue," Nicole said. "He might not reveal things he knows because he doesn't want to slip and make a remark about how he felt about Leslie. He could be playing dumb to hide how obsessed he was with her."

"Good point," Robby said.

"Maybe we should go talk to him again," Claire said.

"I won't be free for a few days," Nicole said. "Remember I have those two wedding cakes to get ready? Maybe you should go speak to Ambrose without me?"

"I think I will," Claire said. "And maybe arriving unannounced would be best."

"Catch the guy off guard." Robby nodded.

The rest of the hour passed with the three workers discussing aspects of the case and speculating about the killer while they finished up the baking. Claire and Robby left the shop at the same time, but each turned in different directions.

"See you tomorrow," Robby told Claire as he hurried off to a class in vocal performance.

Claire fiddled with her bag trying to find her phone when a husky voice called her name. Looking up, she saw a slim, well-dressed man leaning against the wall of the brick building.

"I thought you got out of work at 3pm." The man had jet black hair and wore sunglasses and a dark blue, tweed suit jacket.

Bob Cooney pushed himself off the wall and took a few steps towards Claire. A former private investigator, Cooney had a reputation for being involved in shady dealings and making a bundle off of them. He also had a reputation for knowing lots about things that went on in the city.

"How would you know when I get out of work?" Claire asked. "Do you spy on me?"

"I know things." Cooney, in his mid-fifties, removed a pack of cigarettes from his pocket and lit one of them with a shiny gold lighter.

"What brings you to this neck of the woods?" Claire tilted her head to the side.

"You." Cooney shoved a hand into his pocket as he took a long drag of his cigarette. "Where you headed anyway? I'll walk with you."

"I don't need an escort," Claire frowned.

"I'll walk with you anyway." Cooney fell into step beside Claire as they headed through the financial district towards the Common.

"Why?"

"I got some things to say to you."

"I haven't been to the bank," Claire sassed the man. "So I'm not paying you for unsolicited conversation."

"This one's on me," Cooney said. "Just don't get used to it."

Claire stopped walking and turned to the man, her blue eyes like lasers. "Why? Why is this chat free?"

"I happen to enjoy our occasional question and answer interactions and I thought it might be helpful to keep you out of trouble since I also like the money I make from our little discussions." Claire had approached Cooney twice for information about two cases she was involved with.

"What sort of trouble?" Claire's palms began to feel clammy.

"The kind that can get you killed." Cooney started walking again and Claire hurried after him.

"If you think your comment is going to frighten me into asking you for information so I'll pay you, then you're dead wrong."

Cooney held his hand up. "I'd appreciate it if you don't insult me. You make me sound like all I care about is money."

"Sorry," Claire said. "Forgive me if I haven't yet seen a different side of you."

"That's harsh, Rollins. Here's the thing. You're sticking your nose into old stuff, stuff you might want to keep away from."

"Why would I want to do that?"

"Because some people aren't as upstanding as you are."

"Exactly what are you trying to tell me?" Claire asked the man.

"I heard you had a problem with some red powder on your front steps a few days ago."

Claire's breath caught in her throat. "How do you know that?"

"Word gets around."

Claire asked firmly, "Do you know who killed Leslie Baker?"

"No, I don't," Cooney said. "But some people probably do."

"If someone knows who the killer is, why don't they go to the police?"

Cooney let out a slow breath of air. "Because, like I told you before ... some people don't think like you do."

"If a person knew who killed someone, couldn't that person get the information to the police?"

"They probably could."

"Then why don't they?"

"Because, Rollins, they don't care, they don't give a...."

"Am I in danger?" Claire asked.

"Most likely not ... maybe." Cooney stopped again. "You need to watch your back. You've been lucky in the past, but Lady Luck might stop smiling on you. You got any pepper spray?"

Claire nodded.

"Where is it?"

"In my bag."

Cooney let out an exasperated sigh. "Lot a good that does. What are you going to do if you get attacked? Tell the guy to hold on a minute while you wade through all the junk you got in that purse?"

Claire didn't say anything.

"What are you going to do if I lunge at you? Wrap my hands around your throat?"

"Fight you."

"You'll lose. I guarantee it."

Claire made a face and was about to say something when Cooney said, "I'm going to put my hands around your throat."

"Is that a good idea? We're in a public place. People will think you're attacking me."

Cooney didn't pay attention to Claire's comment and went ahead and placed his hands on her throat. "Try to get my hands away."

Pulling at the man's hands, Claire tried to break his hold on her without success.

Cooney said, "Do this." He moved the young woman's hands, one up between his grasp and the other hand, up around the outside of his arm. "Now, clasp your hands together and use your body weight to pull down on my arm and twist. Twist hard. Do it. Commit to it."

Claire used all of her might to do as she had been directed, and, to her surprise, she broke Cooney's hold on her throat.

"Now you'd run, take off like the devil himself is after you ... because you won't get a second chance." Cooney stuffed his hands into his pockets. "You got it, Rollins? Commit. Fight like hell. Then maybe fortune will go your way."

Claire nodded and asked, "Do you know who put the red powder on my steps?"

"If I did, I'd tell you." Cooney started away down the grassy hill of the Common. "Don't trust anyone. Keep your guard up. Keep those dogs of yours with you, too. And tell that boyfriend of yours to practice self-defense with you."

With a smile, Claire called to him, "You know what? You're a strange man."

Cooney didn't look back. "I'll take that as a compliment."

26

Claire waited in the university's anthropology department for Professor Malden Ambrose to get out of a meeting. The space had a large wooden desk where the receptionist sat and directed students and visitors to the correct office. The department mail boxes were on the wall to the right, a series of divided small shelves with the name of the faculty or staff member above each one. Two upholstered chairs flanked a non-working fireplace and faculty photographs graced the walls with both formal portraits and informal shots of archaeological digs, professors presenting at conferences and giving lectures.

As Claire wandered around glancing at the photos, Ambrose walked briskly into the room heading for his mailbox when he noticed the blond young woman. The man's facial expression lost its easy-going look and he seemed to want to slink away before Claire noticed him.

"Professor Ambrose." Claire smiled and crossed the space to stand near him. "Sorry to drop by unannounced. Do you have a few minutes?"

Ambrose blinked and took a quick look at his watch. "I have a meeting shortly," he stammered.

Claire said, "I promise not to keep you. It will only take a few minutes."

Ambrose looked at the receptionist as if he was fumbling for another excuse and then said, "Come to my office." He led the way down the hall, into his room, and shut the door with a loud click. "Have a seat." Ambrose took the chair behind the desk. "What can I do for you?"

"If you don't mind, I just have a few quick questions to follow up on our previous meeting." Claire leaned back and rested her hands on the arms of the chair.

"Yes?" Ambrose gestured for Claire to go ahead.

"There are still questions about the trowel."

"Why is this trowel garnering such interest?" Ambrose asked impatiently.

"It could have significance to the case," Claire said evenly.

Ambrose shook his head. "What sort of significance?"

"There are many details involved in a case like this, thousands, really," Claire explained. "Many of them need to align in order to point the investigators in the right direction. It takes hours and hours to create a picture of a victim's life, little things, big things, some important, most not so much, but they all come together to help law enforcement."

"What do you want to know?" Ambrose sighed.

"Did you give the trowel to Leslie?" Claire asked.

"I did not."

"Did you have the trowel in your possession after leaving Iraq?"

"I don't recall."

"Some people we've interviewed thought you no longer had the tool after you returned to the States from Iraq."

Ambrose sat up straight, his brow wrinkled. "Who claimed that? Who said that?"

"I'm not allowed to say," Claire told him.

"I don't remember if I had it or not. It was ages ago. Why is this so important?"

"We're trying to figure out if the killer took the trowel from Leslie's apartment," Claire told him.

Ambrose looked stricken. "Why would the killer do that?"

"That's what we're trying to determine," Claire said. "We'd like to locate the trowel."

"You don't even know if Leslie ever had it." Ambrose's eyes bored into Claire. "Do you?"

"Do you have the trowel in your possession?"

"Now? No, I don't."

"Did you have it after Iraq?" Claire asked gently.

"I don't remember."

"Did Leslie ever mention a man named Henry Prior to you?"

Ambrose shook his head in frustration. "It was too long ago. I don't recall specifics of our conversations."

Claire persisted. "Did she ever mention someone who was acting aggressively towards her?"

"Not that I recall."

"Did Leslie give any indications that she used drugs?"

"Drugs?" Ambrose nearly shouted the word. "Absolutely not."

"Did you feel like you knew Leslie well?"

Ambrose rubbed his forehead. "We were together for only a few weeks in Iraq and then we met occasionally for coffee. In all honesty, I can't say I knew her well."

"At the time you were in Iraq, were you happy in your marriage?"

Ambrose stared at Claire. "I'd only been married a short time."

"So you *were* happy?" Claire asked.

"Yes, I was." Ambrose replied as if he were being accused.

"Did Leslie ever indicate to you that she was interested in being more than friends?"

"She did not." Ambrose said the three words through gritted teeth. "And, no, I did not have an affair with her."

"Did anything you said or did give Leslie the impression you would have liked to engage in an affair?"

"I certainly hope not. I was married. Newly married."

"Please know I'm not accusing you of anything. People's relationships are complicated. It wouldn't be a surprise if you were interested in Leslie. She was an attractive and intelligent young woman. We're only trying to build a snapshot of Leslie. Who was important to her, who her friends were, who she might have confided in."

Ambrose's shoulders seemed to relax a little. He gave Claire a nod. "I just don't know the answers to the questions that might help you. It's frustrating not to be of any help."

"Is there anything you recall Leslie saying about Peter Safer, her boyfriend?"

"Nothing important. She barely talked about him."

A knock sounded on the professor's door and when he told the person to come in, the receptionist poked her head in. "The students are here for office hours."

"I'll be free in a moment."

The door closed again and Ambrose stood up. "I have students to meet with now." He walked Claire to the waiting area where the two said goodbye and Ambrose returned to his office.

As Claire passed a couple of students, she overheard one comment on how young Professor Ambrose looked in the photograph on the wall. Claire looked over at the picture the young men were talking about and it reminded her of a snapshot she'd seen in Rosalind Fenwick's photo album.

Ambrose was bent over a lab table that had a

number of artifacts spread over the top of it. His hair was longer and he wore a tight t-shirt and slim jeans. Something was stuck into his back pocket and the handle of the object was jutting out.

A shiver raced through Claire and she was about to step closer to the framed photo to get a better look when two more students crowded around the others to see the picture under discussion.

"Is there anything else you need, Ms. Rollins?" the receptionist asked with a smile.

"Nothing," Claire said as she headed for the door with a quick glance back at the wall photo. "Thank you for your help."

WHEN CLAIRE COLLECTED the Corgis from Tony's shop, the evening employee was the only one working. Tony and Tessa had gone out for dinner and it was too late in the day for Augustus to be at his usual table at the back of the store. Claire's mind was racing and she couldn't wait to get home.

For the past days, whenever she approached her townhouse, a bit of nervousness flashed through her body as she recalled the red powder sprinkled over her stairs. Claire slowed her steps and checked to be sure the path was clear before allowing the dogs to bound up to the front door.

Inside the house, she headed to the desk in the living room, took something from the top of the workspace, and carried it to the sofa. Bear and Lady jumped up next to her and when they saw what she had, they let out loud barks.

"Okay, settle down, you two." With her heart pounding, Claire patted the dogs' heads as she paged through Rosalind Fenwick's old photo album of pictures taken at digs she'd been on.

Claire was sure she'd seen a photograph of Malden Ambrose in the album she held on her lap that was very similar to the picture hanging on the wall in the anthropology department. Flipping the pages, she stopped.

Bear barked three times as Lady pushed at the album with her nose.

Hurrying back to her desk, Claire removed a magnifying glass from the drawer and darted back to the photo where she placed the round glass close to the image.

Claire's head snapped up and her heart skipped a beat. In the back pocket of Ambrose's jeans, the handle of a tool stuck out. The handle looked to have inlays in it … and one of them seemed to be chipped.

Rapidly turning back some of the pages, Claire arrived at the section heading: *France*. The date written alongside the word was five years *after* Leslie had been murdered.

Claire's heart began to race.

Whether or not Leslie took Ambrose's trowel before leaving Iraq or Ambrose gave it to her before she left the dig, how did it end up in Ambrose's back pocket years *after* Leslie had been killed?

27

Claire knew Ian was involved in a stakeout so she didn't want to call him until later and Nicole was busy preparing a wedding cake for the next morning. Claire sent a text to Marty and asked if he was up for her coming by to see him. He replied almost immediately inviting Claire to visit.

After removing the plastic covered page from Rosalind Fenwick's photo album that held the picture of Malden Ambrose, Claire grabbed the dogs' leashes and hitched them to the Corgis' collars. "Come on, dogs, we're going for a walk."

Bear and Lady wagged their little tails and trotted out the door, down the street, past the Common and through the Public Garden to Boylston Street and Marty Wyatt's condo. Once inside the man's place, the dogs greeted him with exuberant wiggling and wagging and dog-kisses on the hand causing Marty to let loose with belly laughs. "I love these dogs."

Marty looked about the same as he had when Claire visited last time, pale, weak, unsteady. Marty said he was now on an experimental drug to help his lung disease and as yet, had not made any improvement.

"Give it time," Claire encouraged.

"Time is something I don't have a lot of," Marty said.

Claire reached into her bag and slipped out the plastic sheet of photos. "I was in the anthropology department to speak with Malden Ambrose again and I noticed a photograph on the wall of the reception area. I tried to get a better look, but students were standing around waiting for office hours." Claire went on to say the picture on the wall reminded her of something she'd seen in Rosalind Fenwick's album. "Here is the photo. It shows Professor Ambrose at a dig in France. If you look closely, you can make out a tool sticking out of his back pocket."

Marty lifted the picture closer to his eyes and he

squinted trying to make out the image of the trowel. "I see what you mean. What is it?"

"I think its Ambrose's trowel ... the one with pearl inlays on the handle. The one that was in Leslie's apartment after she returned from Iraq." Claire locked eyes with Marty. "The one Ambrose claims he doesn't know what happened to it. This photo was taken five years after Leslie was killed. How did that tool end up in Ambrose's pocket if Leslie had it in her room?"

Claire could see Marty's chest rapidly rising and falling as the significance of Ambrose having the trowel hit him.

"How did Ambrose get it back?" Marty's eyes were wide. "He must have been in Leslie's apartment?"

"He told me he had never been in Leslie's place," Claire reported.

"He might be lying. He might have gone there and taken the trowel back," Marty speculated.

"He told me he didn't know what happened to the tool."

Marty's face had paled even more. "Ambrose went to Leslie's apartment, walked in, took the trowel, and killed her?"

Bear let out a loud bark and Lady whined.

Claire jumped from the dog's sudden bark. "It's possible. I think Ambrose was still obsessed with Leslie. I bet he met with her after Iraq to convince her to start seeing him and when she didn't agree, it made him wild. I think Ambrose went to Leslie's apartment to try again. She refused, and in a rage, Ambrose struck her. Ambrose knew ancient cultural burial practices. He understood the importance of sprinkling the body with red powder. I bet he spotted his trowel among Leslie's things and took it."

Marty ran his hand over his face and looked again at the sheet of photographs resting in his lap. "Ambrose has the trowel in this picture, five years after Leslie died. Ambrose must have killed her." Tears formed in Marty's eyes and they dropped onto the plastic that covered the pictures.

Claire hurried over to Marty and put her arm around his shoulders as the man lifted his hand and wiped at his eyes with the cuff of his shirt. "I'm.... I can't believe this might be the answer I've been looking for all these years. Is tonight the beginning of the end of all my searching? Will the case finally be solved?"

"I hope so," Claire whispered as she squeezed Marty's hand. "I hope so."

After making tea and sitting with Marty for

another hour watching night fall over the city and talking over details of the case, Claire received a text from Ian telling her he was on the way to her townhouse. Claire responded by telling him she had some important news to share and couldn't wait to see him. She told him to use the key she'd given him to let himself into her place and she'd be back soon.

Walking in the dark past the Common caused chills of nervousness to rush over Claire's skin making her uneasy and on edge. She kept looking over her shoulders to see if anyone was following her and Bob Cooney's words ran through her mind. *What are you going to do? Ask the attacker to wait while you rummage through that purse of yours?*

Claire stopped the dogs and said, "Wait a second." Dropping her bag at her feet, she pushed her hand around the bottom of the purse until she grabbed her pepper spray. "Okay, let's go," she told the Corgis while she gripped the small canister in her palm.

On the sidewalk outside her townhouse, Bear and Lady began acting agitated ... growling, pulling on the leashes, and whining. As Claire cursed herself for not leaving a light on inside, she wondered where Ian was. Maybe he took a cab?

Claire looked at the windows of her place. None

of the lights were on. She looked up the street and spotted Ian's car parked at the top of the lane. Where is Ian? Why is my house all dark?"

Claire headed for the steps that led to her front door, but then halted. Her heart pounded like a drum against her chest wall. If Ian was inside, why hadn't he turned on a light?

Bear looked up at his owner and whined. Lady tugged on the leash.

"Shhh," Claire told the dogs and they quieted right away. "Let's go around back and see if the lights are on in the kitchen," she whispered.

The young woman and her dogs hurried a little way down the sidewalk, entered the side alley, and pushed through some bushes to make it around behind the white fence that enclosed her tiny yard. Claire squatted and pushed at the loose slat in the fence so she could peek at the rear of her townhouse. It was completely dark.

"This isn't good," she told the Corgis as her stomach sank. "This isn't good at all." Fear gripped her so tightly, she felt like she couldn't breathe. Claire removed her keys from her bag and clutched the pepper spray in her hand. Making sure the slat was pushed to the side, she abandoned her purse behind the fence, and then led the dogs back to the alley to a spot she judged to be equidistant from both the front door and the back of the townhouse.

Claire looked down at the dogs and raised her arm, pointing to where they'd just come from. "Ready? Go find Ian. Go get him," she shouted. The dogs raced back to the opening in the fence.

And then Claire took off for the front of the house.

RUNNING up the steps to her door, Claire could hear Bear and Lady barking like rabid animals as she shoved her key in the lock and gently pushed the door open. She held her breath and quietly closed the door. Hugging the shadows for a moment, she stood listening to the hullabaloo the dogs were making at the sliding glass doors to the living room. *Good dogs.*

Claire attempted to slow her breathing as she tried to sense the movement of someone's feet or someone's presence close to her. She wanted to call out for Ian, but since he hadn't let the dogs in, he either wasn't inside or he was....

Claire wouldn't finish her thought.

All she wanted to do was dissolve into a puddle

on the floor. Fear felt like it was filling her stomach with ice water and as her vision became more accustomed to the darkness, everything seemed to be swimming before her eyes.

Still gripping her pepper spray, Claire jammed her fingernails into her palms trying to throw off her panic and dizziness. She focused on taking in one deep breath and then letting it out. After three breaths, she slipped her feet over the floor to make her way to the kitchen.

Bear and Lady were jumping up and down outside the sliding door, growling and barking like maniacs.

A shaft of moonlight came in from the door and pooled on the living room floor ... and Claire saw Ian's legs illuminated by the light. Her boyfriend was on his back on the floor.

With a gasp, Claire rushed to Ian's side and kneeled next to him, her hand touching the side of his face. Blood pooled under his head. "Ian?" The word came out like a sob.

Despite the barking frenzy of the dogs, Claire froze when she heard the heavy scuff of a shoe on the wood floor. She wheeled to see Malden Ambrose standing in the living room and a shudder of déjà vu raced through her veins as she recalled a previous case when the perpetrator broke into the townhouse and threatened her.

"You." Claire scrambled to her feet, rage bubbling up in her chest. "You hurt Ian."

"Shut up," Ambrose sneered.

Claire lifted her eyes to Ambrose. "You killed Leslie." Her voice was as sharp as a knife.

"Too bad you didn't keep your nose out of it. Then no one else would've gotten hurt." Ambrose took a step closer.

While Claire tried to gauge whether her pepper spray would reach Ambrose's face, the man lunged at her. She jabbed the top of the spray canister with her thumb, but the liquid overshot the mark and missed Ambrose. The man took full advantage of the spray's misdirection and he wrapped his hands around Claire's throat like an iron vise.

Ambrose's eyes blazed and his face contorted as he choked Claire with such force that she was sure her neck bones would snap. Panicking, she flailed at the man's arms and scratched at his hands and face. The Corgis wildly clawed at the glass door just yards away from Claire and the sound of their howls dimmed as her hearing started to fade.

Bob Cooney's words began to play in her head. *Use your body weight. Twist. Commit. Fight like hell.*

Maybe fortune's wheel had not yet decided where it would stop.

With a burst of desperation, Claire clasped her hands together the way Cooney had instructed, lifted her feet off the floor and yanked down and around trying to break the hold on her throat. Contracting the muscles in her right leg, Claire used her last bit of energy to punch her foot into Ambrose's knee.

The man's leg bent backwards from the impact of Claire's shoe on the knee and Ambrose screeched in pain as his hands lost their grip and he fell backwards onto the floor. Claire sprang towards the sliding glass door, grasped at the lock, and pushed it open allowing the dogs to burst in. Growling, they ran at Ambrose and were on him in two seconds.

Claire dove for her pepper spray, grabbed it, and pushed herself up, wheezing and gasping for air and she stood bent over watching the Corgis' attack on the man.

Ambrose thrashed and screamed and, at last, Claire had enough breath to call off the dogs. Rushing to Ian with tears streaming down her face, she searched frantically at his neck for a pulse and her heart leapt with joy when she felt his heart beat against her fingers.

Claire pulled Ian's cell phone from his pocket and punched the buttons to make the emergency call, then she lovingly ran her hand along the side of his face before struggling to her feet and hobbling over to be sure Ambrose wasn't attempting to make an escape. She need not have worried.

Bear and Lady stood watch over the professor who was still writhing in pain on the living room floor and if he moved too much, the dogs let out menacing growls and snaps.

While she waited for the ambulance and the police to arrive, Claire clutched her pepper spray in one hand, and with the other, pressed a towel to Ian's head wound to stop the bleeding. With a groan, he blinked a few times and looked up at Claire with groggy eyes.

"It's okay," she whispered tenderly. "I'm here. We're together. Help is on the way."

28

Professor Malden Ambrose confessed to the thirty-three-year old murder of Leslie Baker. Ambrose panicked when Claire persisted in her questions about the trowel and decided she was getting too close to discovering he was the killer. He was also the one who sprinkled the red powder over Claire's front steps.

Leslie Baker took the trowel from Ambrose's things a few days before leaving Iraq. Why she took it remained a mystery. Some speculated Leslie wanted to get back at Ambrose for aggressively coming on to her so she stole his trowel as a way to thumb her nose at him.

After returning from the Iraq dig, Ambrose often called Leslie to invite her to meet for coffee or dinner or drinks. On occasion, Leslie agreed to meet the professor for coffee and each time, Ambrose suggested a liaison and the young woman refused.

Ambrose was so obsessed with Leslie and furious that she told him she wouldn't meet with him anymore that one night he arrived late at her building and entered her apartment after trying the doorknob and finding it unlocked.

He told police that he found Leslie in bed, reading. She was agitated that he had arrived unannounced which only served to further infuriate him. Leslie repeated that she would not engage in an affair with the man and when she started to leave the room, Ambrose struck her with a paperweight he found on her bookcase. He dragged her to the bed where he continued to strike her until she was dead. Ambrose covered Leslie with items from the room, a blanket, a rug, a coat. He had no explanation for why he'd done that.

On his way out, he spotted the ochre Leslie used in her painting and decided to sprinkle it over the body as was the custom of some ancient cultures. Ambrose saw his trowel on the shelf of the young woman's bookcase and he grabbed it, took the paperweight, and left the building.

Claire visited Marty Wyatt at his condo to discuss

the case details and Ambrose's confession to murder. Marty had a bit of color in his cheeks and had more energy than usual. He even made the tea for himself and Claire and carried it to the coffee table by the big windows.

"The new drugs are having a positive impact," Marty announced. "I have a better appetite. I'm more optimistic." He smiled at Claire. "Maybe Lady Luck is shining down on me."

"Well," Claire said, "she must be because your cold case is solved and now you're feeling better. Things are turning around."

"I haven't felt this good in a hundred years," Marty told Claire causing her to laugh at his exaggeration.

"I'm so glad." Claire's eyes sparkled at the kind man and she hoped that he would recover enough from his disease to live for years to come. "When you came to my house the night Nicole was there ... I was sure you had something you wanted to tell us. Now that the case is solved, are you able to talk about what you wanted to discuss with us?"

Marty ran his hand over the top of his head. "It's nothing earth-shattering, but you're right. I did plan to share something with you. I was sure I didn't have long to live and I didn't want to go to my grave with no one knowing."

Claire tilted her head. "Knowing? Knowing what?"

"Why I have been chasing this murder case for so many years."

"It wasn't because it was the first case you were assigned to report on as a journalist?" Claire asked.

"It was partly that, yes, but there was another reason." Marty set down his mug and breathed a long sigh. "I met Leslie Baker. It was two days before she was killed."

Claire's eyes widened.

"I was new to the area. I didn't know anyone. I was feeling lonely and depressed and like a fish out of water so I went to a pub in Harvard Square to get out of my tiny, empty apartment."

Claire waited for him to go on.

"There was a group of young people standing at the bar talking and laughing. I remember how heavy my loneliness felt." Marty took a deep breath. "I was kind of shy back then, but I figured, what did I have to lose, so I headed over to talk to them. Leslie was in the group. She was so lively and happy and just full of good cheer. It made me feel better just to be next to her. We chatted, she drew me into the group. I had a great time. Leslie invited me to a party in her building for the next weekend. I went home feeling good, like I was making friends." Marty looked over at Claire. "Leslie was nice to me."

"Why did you feel the need to keep the information secret?" Claire asked.

"At the time, I was afraid I might become a suspect. It was a foolish fear, but I was scared. People saw me with Leslie two nights prior to her death. I have to admit I had a crush on her from that night. I didn't know she had a boyfriend. I guess she didn't consider Peter her boyfriend at that time. It was one of their off-again times. I met my future wife about a month after Leslie was killed. I never told her I had a crush on Leslie. It didn't seem right to tell her."

Marty went on. "The kindness Leslie showed me never left my heart. It spurred me to search for her killer, to bring her a measure of justice. I wanted her to know someone was still trying to find the person who took her life. I wanted her to know I hadn't forgotten her." Marty batted at his eyes.

"You did it, Marty," Claire said softly. "You never gave up. Without your persistence, the case would never have been solved. I'm sure Leslie is smiling down on you."

Marty had a faraway look on his face.

"It's strange, isn't it?" Claire asked. "Fate, chance encounters, the way fortune's wheel turns for each one of us. If you hadn't met Leslie that night, Ambrose would still be free. The killer probably never would have been caught."

CLAIRE RESTED next to Ian in his hospital bed, the two of them watching the small television attached to a metal arm that swung out from the wall. Ian had suffered a nasty smash on the head that required stitches and he had a concussion. The doctor wanted him to stay one more night for observation, and if all looked good, he would be released in the morning with orders to stay out of work for at least two weeks.

Claire gently ran her hand over the side of Ian's face.

"Don't stop," Ian told his girlfriend as he squeezed her other hand. "Don't ever stop."

Claire smiled. "I'll tell Nicole I won't be able to work at the shop for the next two weeks in order to stroke your face to speed your recovery."

"Fine with me," Ian said and slid a little closer to Claire.

Ian had arrived at Claire's townhouse the night

Ambrose planned to kill her. He used his key to go inside and disarmed the burglar alarm. Ambrose darted up the front steps and pushed his way inside before Ian had a chance to shut the door. Surprising Ian, he bashed the detective on the head, knocking him out.

Through the front window, Ambrose saw Claire and the dogs arriving home and he dragged Ian into the living room with plans to finish him off, but Claire had snuck around back and Ambrose heard her say something to the dogs. Ambrose temporarily abandoned the plan to kill Ian and hid in the bedroom waiting for Claire to come inside.

"I'm starving," Ian said reaching for the remote to change the channel. "This hospital food isn't doing it for me."

As soon as he said those words, Tony, Tessa, Nicole, and Augustus walked through the door into Ian's room.

"I never expected to see you flattened," Tony told the man.

Ian laughed. "The only thing flattened is my head."

"We brought you food," Tessa announced. "And flowers and candy and...."

Augustus removed a bottle of beer from the

pocket of his overcoat and, with a grin, set it on the table next to Ian. "And some alcohol."

Nicole carried a brown pastry box. "I brought your favorite cheesecake."

Ian adjusted the pillow behind his back and straightened. "I should get hit in the head more often."

Tony had a cooler in his hand and he unzipped the top of it and removed a large pan of lasagna. "I'll find a place to warm this up and then we'll fill that empty stomach of yours."

Nicole, with her dark hair flowing around her shoulders, sat on the foot of the bed. "We devised a plan to sneak the Corgis in to see you, but at the last minute, we realized it would never work. So Bear and Lady had to send their love to you and hope you're out of here soon."

"Tell those magnificent animals thank you and I'll see them tomorrow."

Nicole said, "Oh, and Robby had a class so he couldn't come with us, but he's making you a batch of chocolate-caramel cookies and will deliver them to you tomorrow."

At the visitors' request, Ian told the story of Ambrose's attack on him and how Claire had saved him.

"I really didn't." Claire pushed a strand of hair from Ian's forehead.

"You certainly did," Ian said. "Your quick thinking and self-defense skills saved the day ... and my life."

"Hmm," Claire leaned over and gave Ian a kiss. "I'll have to think of a way you can repay me."

Claire had already planned to visit Bob Cooney at the South End bar he frequented to thank him for giving her the tips to use on an attacker. She was even going to bring him a sampler of desserts from the chocolate shop to show her gratitude.

Tony walked back in with a warmed plate of lasagna for Ian. "If you ask nicely, you often get what you need. A very kind nurse helped me get the food warmed up." He put a towel over Ian's chest and set the plate on the wheeled table that could be pushed up right over Ian's lap.

"It smells awfully good in here." A tall, athletic, sandy-haired man stepped into the hospital room and when he saw the group gathered around Ian, he offered to return later.

"This is Dr. Foley, my neurologist." Ian introduced the doctor to his friends and when Foley shook hands with Nicole, his eyes almost bugged from their sockets.

"Why don't you go ahead and eat," Dr. Foley suggested and then he eagerly started a conversation with Nicole while the others chattered away at Ian.

Sitting next to her boyfriend while he enjoyed his lasagna, Claire watched the sparks fly between her best friend and the neurologist.

Fate, chance meetings.

A little smile formed over Claire's mouth as the neurologist beamed at Nicole and Nicole's eyes sparkled at the good-looking, young doctor.

Fortune's wheel was turning.

THANK YOU FOR READING!

Books by J.A. WHITING can be found here:
www.amazon.com/author/jawhiting

To hear about new books and book sales, please sign up for my mailing list at:
www.jawhitingbooks.com

Your email will never be sold, shared, or spammed.

If you enjoyed the book, please consider leaving a review. A few words are all that's needed. It would be very much appreciated.

BOOKS/SERIES BY J. A. WHITING

**CLAIRE ROLLINS COZY MYSTERY SERIES*

**PAXTON PARK COZY MYSTERIES*

**LIN COFFIN COZY MYSTERY SERIES*

**SWEET COVE COZY MYSTERY SERIES*

**OLIVIA MILLER MYSTERY-THRILLER SERIES (not cozy)*

ABOUT THE AUTHOR

J.A. Whiting lives with her family in New England. Whiting loves reading and writing mystery stories.

Visit me at:

www.jawhitingbooks.com

www.facebook.com/jawhitingauthor

www.amazon.com/author/jawhiting

Made in the USA
Coppell, TX
25 October 2024

39163680R00177